MIRRORS

MIRRORS

PENNED INFLUENCES

VOL 1

ANDREW D SHEPHERD

Columbus, Ohio

Penned Influences Vol 1: Mirrors

Published by Gatekeeper Press
2167 Stringtown Rd, Suite 109
Columbus, OH 43123-2989
www.GatekeeperPress.com

ISBN: 9781619848252

Printed in the United States of America

Contact the author at pennedproductions@gmail.com
For additional information, visit us at www.pennedproductions.com

MOTHERS FOR MIRRORS

Vikki Ammons

Newport News, Virginia

*"Don't ask anyone to open a door you're not willing
to walk through."*

People oftentimes look for others to help them. This [passage] prepares young men in my life to only ask if they're really truly ready to move forward and progress in life!! It reminds them if they ask for an open door, by faith, they will get it...so be careful what you ask for and be ready when you ask for it!!

Juanessa Lucas

Pinehurst, North Carolina

*"If your determination outweighs your fears, if your resolve
can resist the resources of excuses, than your problems cannot
stop your progress."*

I would share these very impactful words with my own. (They) possess the ability to transform a man's fear into courage, relent into fight, complacency into desire, and hopelessness into a world of fulfilled dreams

Taneisha Brown

Washington DC

"When people fail to see your greatness, pity their vision never your reflection"

I believe this passage is so important to men with vision. So many times we are told that something is not possible and we choose to believe others opinions over our vision usually because we trust them more than we trust ourselves. We don't recognize that it was not given to them but given to you. How could they believe or see something that wasn't placed in them. As a mom to a male, my hope is that my son never allows someone to talk him out of bringing forth everything that's placed in him.

Allison Moore

Hampton, Virginia

"Don't ask anyone to open a door, if you're unready to walk thru it."

That is positively influential because it reminds young men to be prepared before you ask for favors and etc. It teaches the lesson of first impressions and it drives home the value in "you often times only get one time to make a statement and if you aren't ready when it's your time, you may not ever get that opportunity again." I think this lesson is incredibly important for young men (and women and old ones too) to understand. Get prepared before the opportunity. Don't wait until the opportunity to get prepared.

Patricia Price Spencer

Arizona

"Your talent and abilities were purchased with an unwritten obligation to never stop trying—an obligation to your creator."

It is important for our young men to know that those who came before us paid a price for them to have the freedom and privileges they often take for granted...it inspires young men to walk the path that was paved by others.

Aisha Ringham

Hampton, Virginia

"Being true to yourself may not mean being true to the person you are now, but to the person you are meant to be, the person you are designed to be."

I would say to my son...your right now is a milestone and you must know your purpose. It is critical that you do not become stagnant and live out the standard, remember -knowing your purpose matters. When one knows their purpose that's all the drive, fuel, motivation and difference. Walls come down, mountains fall and the universe compliments it; then you will be the person you were designed to be.

Tonya Prince

Kaiserslautern, Germany

Inspiring and encouraging. They each (ideals and passages) spoke volumes to me...You cannot move into your future holding on to your past. Those things which cause you to suffer have made you who you are but do not determine who you are meant to be. You cannot move into a better place if you have not figured out where you yet stand. A woman cannot teach a man to be a man for she is not a man, but she can certainly teach him how to treat a woman. Letting go of selfish desires will open your eyes to things you would have never seen. Love lost is not love forgotten, never lose sight of what love really is. Don't be afraid to start over, you've already done it once now you have the opportunity to do it again better.

Tara Thomas

Newport News, Virginia

"Excuses are escape plans for anyone expecting an easy win."

As a mother, I always express to my children that I do not accept excuses, either get it done or find a way. I am very firm with discipline with my children. I express to my son and daughter, the world is a very hard and demanding place . . . .especially for our African American children. Despite what some may believe, my children were born with a gift and a curse. They were created to stand out and to live out the paths our Lord has laid out for them, BUT they also have more obstacles to overcome. My job as a parent is to teach and prepare my children for this crazy word. It starts by not accepting excuses but accepting solutions to all and any problems they may intercede in life.

Joi Rice

Fort Leonard Wood, Missouri

"Turning frustration into positive action is fire worth burning. Without action, it only burns you"

I've had many a days where I've been frustrated because something didn't go according to plan but I never let that stop be, that frustration was fuel for me to dig deeper, find another way and continue to journey towards my destination

Tamina Laudat

Yorktown, Virginia

"Waiting for an opportunity before preparing is waiting to win the lottery without buying a ticket."

Like the good book says, "Faith without works is dead." This would explain to my teenage brother, God has blessed you with wisdom and the tools necessary to make things happen. All it takes is a leap of faith, passion and hard work. Everyone will tell you no, but god will always tell you yes.

Lakota Copeland

Southern Pines, North Carolina

"Your setbacks doesn't have to set you back."

You may be experiencing a challenging moment at the time, but it does not mean that you will remain there forever. Dust yourself off, pray, and get back out there to conquer your goal(s). Stare any uncertainty and your fears in the face while remaining steadfast and headstrong.

Dee Robinson

Newport News, Virginia

"Lead your generation into the future, but be prepared to leave some of your generation in the past."

My son is 22 years old and I believe this would benefit him to know that living is not just about the moment but about legacy. You have an obligation to yourself and future generations be learn, grow, evolve and give back so others have a chance.

CONTENTS

"Teary eyes produce unclear vision.
Unclear vision lead to missed opportunities.
Who among us can afford missed opportunities?
Prison yards are littered with the fallen branches of our family trees,
we're fighting against the ropes, we're even fighting the referees.
But me must stop fighting we, and we must stop polluting us.
Raging a war on influences is more vital than any war on drugs.
So there can be no relenting in addressing all such devices.
For at the core, our most severe crises, is only an identity crisis."

INTRODUCTION

I T MAY HAVE been someone's home I was breaking into but it was really only a line, a line I was about to cross. I didn't realize it at the time, but I was crossing it alone. There were no voices in my ear, not even mine. The voice I had on the inside could've been a guide, but after ignoring him for so long, he was gone, too, leaving me with only the voices of the boys I was trying to impress. It's funny when thinking about it now. My environment never really impressed me. Nothing I saw outside of my window or on the news was impressive, but I spent so much of myself trying to impress it. My environment was who I was, who I thought I was.

So many of my decisions were based on who I thought I was, like the decision to get in their truck and the decision to jump the man's fence and ultimately, break into his house. I don't know why I thought it was okay to play a part in all of it, but I kept playing. But when it was really show time, I realized I was playing the lead role in someone else's story.

Once we were in the house, it was clear who the leader *was*, and it was not me. I was afraid to touch anything. When they looked to me to get the thievery-party started, I hid my fear by pretending that I didn't see anything I wanted to steal. My elementary football coach used to say fear was contagious, but mine wasn't. My boys stole everything they saw. Seeing them fill their coat pockets and pants legs was what encouraged me to keep the party going. That's when I saw the watch.

1

I never thought stealing time would cost me time. I wasn't actually losing time; I was giving it away—a year of my life to the Juvenile Detention Center.

Not because I took the watch but because of what I didn't take— the opportunities to turn back. There were so many of them and they were all staring at me in the face.

That was not the first time I've seen eyes like those. I saw them at home years before I would earn them, before the JDC became my home and ISS became my second home; my brother had them. They were eyes of someone walking off a ledge with his eyes open. I saw Malik with them every time he snuck out the house.

"Where are you going?" "Why do you have to go right now?" Questions I probably annoyed him with over a hundred times when mom use to work nights. Trapping an older brother with stupid questions can be easy when it's just you and him. When his friends started meeting him at home after school, a little brother's concern becomes easier to brush away.

"Go watch TV" was usually the last thing I heard before the door shut behind him. I guess he felt that I was still watching him because he would glance back towards the house as they drove away. After a while they stopped looking back. Sometimes he had hesitation in his eyes before walking out the door at night. After a while, that stopped, too.

Mirrors

This was years before meeting my court assigned mentor, Mr. Solomon, or seeing the visions and hearing the voices that changed my life. And even though I didn't know what it was, I could see when my brother's inner voice was telling him to stop before he made a mistake. I could also see when it stopped. It was in his face. Making the wrong decisions use to look like jumping off a porch, but became as easy as using the steps. "Casual Catastrophes" is what someone later called it. I called it life, but my mom called it stupidity.

It would later make sense for her to look at me the way she did. After a while, my aunts didn't bother to look my way at all. I guess that made sense, too. I learned that being a disappointment is only disappointing if you have expectations; I didn't have any. Not the kind they had. My mother and her sisters were all college graduates. My sister, Patrice, was rolling down that same lane. It all seemed so perfect for her, as if she was a bowling ball being rolled safely down a lane with kiddy rails while I was tossed down a road of speed bumps and quicksand. But that wasn't the case at all—I had to learn that.

I had to learn my sister only had safety rails because she was willing to actually use them and appreciated them. I thought they were just in the way, something holding me back instead of holding me up. After knocking them down and trampling over them enough, I couldn't tell they were ever even there. No one else could either.

"You've been taught better!" became a constant slogan in my house during my junior high years. Having her parenting skills questioned in the principal's office was as last-straw as last-straws could get. But my mom wasn't the only one running out of patience with me. Junior high sports were the high point of being a pre-teen, and before my mom could take me off the basketball team, the coach beat her to it. All the begging in the world didn't allow me to keep my basketball jersey.

"No matter how fast you are, you can't outrun consequences, Terrell," said Mr. Blue.

"I was only selling cigarettes, Coach. Don't you smoke?"

Probably wasn't the best question to ask, but I was desperate. I really wanted to play my eighth-grade year and the lecturing didn't stop with him.

"Did you expect nothing to happen in return, Terrell? Do you ever expect any consequences?"

"It's all good, Ma. I'll just play ball in high school. Later for this reading rainbow, middle school stuff."

"That's your problem. You always think there's a later waiting on you. The rules aren't going to change Terrell—not for you they won't. Conform or be confined, you remember that security person telling you that. He wasn't just talking to be talking."

He might as well have been talking just to be talking as far as I was concerned, my mom too. I wasn't trying to hear what she was talking about. That was for my sister, I thought. I learned that what I wanted to know was from people who are doing what I wanted to do, which were girls and money. If it didn't teach me a faster way of achieving that, I didn't think I needed to know it. What I did know was that working all day at the hospital then going to school all night wasn't something I could learn from, especially with who I was then, or who I thought I was.

So many things went along with who I thought I was. What I watched, what I listened to, the way I dressed, and how people looked at me were just some of things that went into that person I thought I was. And there was a simple but important thing to learn about not being the young man I was supposed to be; who I am today will have to pay the consequences of the person I was pretending to be yesterday. This proved to be true so many times.

One of the first times was when the "Trap" music I was listening to had me believing that life was real. Believing that was the *trap*. Andre and Jerome were two boys trying to live that life in my junior high school. Even though they weren't really from the hood, selling boxes of cigarettes in the hallways and beside wall lockers was risky enough to attract followers. And it made those two more money than the rest of us had, easy money. Getting off the bus, I remember walking through clouds of cigarette smoke on the way to school and hearing Andre say, "That's us, Terrell. All of that smoke, that's money in our pockets and could be money in your pockets too."

They didn't know me like that, but they remembered seeing my older brother, Malik doing similar stuff with their older brothers and cousins. For Malik, it didn't stop with just selling Newports. Coming home with tens and twenties wasn't enough, especially once a few high school guys started flashing the clothes and jewelry that only drug money could buy. My mom saw me going down that same path and some of the teachers saw it too.

"How much did you make, Terrell?" she asked me.

"What, Mrs. Howard?" I responded while trying to slide a five-dollar bill into my pocket without her noticing it. But of course she noticed it. She noticed a lot more than just me stuffing money in my pocket.

"Was it worth your name, Terrell?" "My name?"

"However much you made from selling drugs in this school, was it worth your good name? Because I can promise you, your name won't be good for a long time now."

"Na, Mrs. Howard. Aint nobody selling drugs. Just cigarettes." "That's all?"

"Yes, ma'am, that's all" I said with a smile of relief on my face.

"So you're selling cancer instead of hallucinations. That's supposed to make you blameless? Half of my students are walking down the hallways smelling like smoke. Now I know exactly who to blame. And exactly who to tell."

She saw my face change and she knew why it changed. Most teachers assumed our parents handled our bad behavior, but the teachers in my school had a few front-row seats when it came to how my mother handled me. Causing her to miss work never earned me the benefit of getting punished in private.

"I'll pick up every cigarette butt on campus, I swear, Mrs. Howard. Just don't send for her."

Mrs. Howard was nice enough to stand there and listen to me as I ask for a second chance. She even picked up the five dollars I balled up and dropped on the floor.

"You sold your good name for this, Terrell. Might as well keep it. As far as another chance goes, I would need an accountant to keep up with all the *second* chances I've given you. I can't afford my own accountant, Terrell. And you can't afford any more second chances. One day you may stand in front of someone who's only interested in who you seem to be now, not who you could be tomorrow."

I wasn't worried about some future day; I was just worried about my mom driving to that school. My tomorrows felt guaranteed, so I had time for that, too. But less than a year later, a date came that made my tomorrow's feel less guaranteed—my first court date. That was the day no one wanted to hear my excuses. The judge didn't even ask me to speak. The sheet of paper he was holding told him the only story he was interested in, the only story that counted. So I stood there listening to him describing the boy I spent years pretending to be and watching all those tomorrows I assumed I had vanish quicker than the cigarette smoke I contributed to in middle school.

"A diploma or a criminal record, one of those will be your first biography, Terrell. You choose what they read about you . . ." was a part of a long speech my mother gave during the ride home after I was suspended for selling cigarettes. Cigarettes had nothing to do with why I was in court, but everything else about me did. I wondered if she thought about that speech while we watched the judge read how I was accused of trespassing and theft. I sure thought about it. I thought about a lot of things. I thought about what people tried to tell me and why I didn't listen. Listening took energy, I realized. Trying to understand what makes perfect sense to an experienced grown-up wasn't as easy as not listening at all. So I usually didn't.

"They just don't get it," was the easier way of making sense of it. So that's what I told myself.

Well, they all got it in JUVIE, the Juvenile Detention Center (JDC). Everyone there understood me and agreed with me, too. Nobody said "man up" or "stop making excuses." Everybody was guilty but nobody was wrong, is how we looked at it. And I tried not to notice how some of the guards were looking at us. They were older, the older version of us. I thought that was why they hated on us most of the time, because they were older and their time had passed. I was wrong. They were just tired of seeing full "slave ships" coming in every month. That's what they called the transport buses that brought the offenders in.

"Every seat full?" a guard at the entrance would yell. "Every seat full!" a driver would always yell back.

I could tell he gave up hoping there would be some empty seats on that bus. And we definitely didn't care. More people just gave us more games during the basketball tournaments. That was another problem in our thinking that the attendants (guards) saw and we didn't—the bigger picture. Especially Mr. Bob or "Bible" Bob, as we called him behind his back. Bible Bob saw everything for what it really was.

"They toss a few balls on the court and you forget that this time tomorrow you'll will be outside in the sun, picking trash off the sidewalks,"

"Community service ain't no thing, Mr. Bob. That and basketball is the only time we can move around in this place," I responded thinking he would then let us get back to our game. No such luck.

"So playing games and cleaning the streets are all you young men are good for?"

"What are we supposed to do?" I asked, "break out of here? Find the underground Juvenile railroad and escape?"

Everyone except Mr. Bob laughed as he slowly walked onto the court. I knew then our game just took a long time- out.

"Yes," he growled with his usual mouth full of sunflower seeds. "I expect all of you to break out of here—with your minds. Stop thinking like delinquents and you will be free. Get your minds out of here and your narrow behinds will follow sooner than you think."

"And then what?" another boy asked.

Andrew D Shepherd

"Any little thing we do will just land us right back in here. I've been here three times already."

"There's no temptation uncommon to man, boy! You think those policemen are setting traps just for you? You're not that special to them! People been falling into those same traps for years. But many chose to avoid them. You just chose to keep falling. When are you going to become a man and choose to stand?"

"I am standing!"

"You're not standing; you're just propped up by all the other excuse-makers behind you. Step away from them and become an individual. See if you can hold your own self up."

It wasn't easy ignoring Mr. Bob's sermon and returning to a game of basketball, but by the time we all got to the ages of junior high and high schoolers, most of us had a lot of practice ignoring good advice. We all had mothers or grandmothers who made sure we went to church on Sundays, but it wasn't like the message from church went home with us. Most of us took home the same message we went into church with, "Get money, get girls, and get paid."

That was our theme music and we shared it with our friends, classmates, and everyone we were connected with. An hour of hearing some preacher talk wasn't going to replace that. But I would soon hear from more than just preachers, parents and detention guards. Guidance would come from people I've never seen and some I've never even heard of. They were people who came before me and just as their actions changed our past, their words would change my future.

CHAPTER ONE

"It's not the load that breaks you down,
it's the way you carry it"

—*Lena Horne*

BEFORE THE VISIONS and voices came, the first new voice I heard came at a time when all I expected to hear was my mother. I was denied parole from the detention center after returning the last time and my mom was nowhere to be found. Her encouragement was usually the first thing I heard after those hearings but not that day. I heard an older voice instead, a much deeper voice. "Revolving doors must eventually stop and since you keep returning, it seems it's better they keep you here."

I don't know who he was but he definitely wasn't who I wanted to talk to.

It became even more obvious it didn't matter what I wanted anymore. After putting my college educated mother through the embarrassment of having a repeat offender as her son, nobody cared what I wanted. Watching me leave Junior High school for Juvenile Detention instead of high school wasn't easy for her. It broke some of her heart. When I didn't seem to care about being such a disappointment that broke the rest of it.

The rest of my family stopped trying around that time. They didn't visit anymore either. It became the story of my dad all over again. But instead of having an affair, I was cheating against the "standard of excellence" my aunt kept on about. The standard they use to tell me to learn from my older sister. But at twelve and thirteen years old, I wasn't trying to be like her. I wasn't trying to be like any of them. I was alright with earning my stripes in the system.

Bouncing back and forth from the JDC wasn't a big deal after a while. It was an expectation-free zone, and I loved that about it. The only school work they gave us was enough to keep us busy. The whole "Idle minds, devil's workshop" theory. We were ok with it if they were. Things only stopped being ok when someone asked what putting puzzles together have to do with getting us ready to return to gen-pop (what we called general population or regular school)? Those kinds of questions made dinner time come sooner and lights out come earlier.

But soon something else came, something none of us really knew how to feel about. A new mentorship program—a way to show the city the JDC was doing all they could for us. At first, it was cool having different groups of guys coming to the JDC. It gave us a break from the regular attendants. They all thought sports were the best way to get our attention and they were right. Basketball became an everyday thing. They were clocking their volunteer hours and we got a break from whatever pretend school work they had us doing. Sometimes they even brought food. The first time one of the church groups brought Popeyes chicken, we were licking our fingers for a week. Juvi food is horrible and barely enough to feed a kindergartner. Instead of getting scared straight, I thought they were trying to starve us straight. But the food and basketballs didn't come out every day. Eventually, they wanted to talk to us. Not just to joke around, but really talk to us.

"We can't get you all to stop talking to save our lives, but now you're quiet as mice," was what one of the attendants yelled during an earlier group discussion the mentors were trying to have with us.

"How ya'll gonna be some shy thugs? Those two words don't even belong together," he said laughing with some of the other guards. Some of the mentors were laughing, too, but not all of them. Especially Mr. Solomon, who would change my life.

"A lot of words don't belong together, Sir, like 'thugs' and these young men here. So, calling them that is probably a practice that should be unpracticed," Mr. Solomon said.

"Easy bruh, it's tense enough around here. We try to keep it relaxed."

"Relaxed? When you see a young lion relaxed in the cage, the zoo keeper has won. We don't want zookeepers to win with these young lions . . . do we?"

I never heard anyone talk like that, especially about us. He wasn't from here like the rest of the mentors. And that's how they started treating him. Mr. Solomon didn't get picked up during any of the mentor/ mentee basketball games and no one ever asked him to be their Spades partner. But he was always there, with a serious look on his face. Not upset or mad, but concerned.

But some of the mentors were alright with the attendants and alright with us too. Most of them were former high school sports legends and others belonged to some church. Even the church guys claimed to be legends on the basketball courts. Sam Nathans was one of those legends. He was my friend Daquan's mentor. Sam talked a good one like the rest of them, until we got him on the court and found out the truth. But Sam still was alright with us. He was assigned to Quan when Quan's parents got worried about him going back to the streets. Sam didn't just shoot ball with us, he listened. He listened to our plans of opening a Barber Shop.

Corner Cuts was going to be our spot. Quan had enough practice from cutting his little brother's hair. There were no men in my family, but I learned how to give myself fades in the mirror. Sam encouraged it big time. He convinced the staff to let him bring some clippers one visit to let Quan trim him up. It was tight. After that, he talked about bussing future generations of Juvi kids to our shop to get professional style haircuts, for job interviews, and serious stuff like that. We liked those kind of conversations. Hearing some of us talking about things that didn't include sports, music, or crime was new. It made being normal not seem so much like losing to some of us.

11

Some of us still had NFL and NBA dreams, even after hearing enough mentors and church deacons tell us to be realistic. But Mr. Sam was on some reach for the stars type stuff. He had Quan thinking he could be the Carolina Panther's starting running back and team barber at the same time. But soon the team would break up.

"I'll be back before you know it, man. But hopefully to just visit this time." he said while leaving the JDC for the last time.

Mr. Sam believed we were both good kids and tried keeping us together the best he could.

"Tight brothers leaves less room for others" was how he explained it when he brought Daquan back to see me after he was released. Dequan and I were both in for the same crime but it was Quan's first time in the system, which made his parole an easier sell for the judge. Especially with an ex-cop like Mr. Sam speaking on his behalf. After a while Quan felt close to Sam but he didn't live with Sam. Quan lived off of Merchansin Rd. The "Merc." We all learned early on—"the Merc hurts." Even with it's reputation, those that lived on Merchansin Rd used it as a neighborhood bragging right.

For us in Juvi, we didn't have much to brag about besides scoring points on the courts or scoring with some girls, but Quan had his shoe collection. His uncle had a hook up at some sports store and Quan was his only nephew. I was jealous of that for a long time. He knew his mom would have a fresh pair waiting for him when he got out. Unfortunately, one night he wore them at the wrong time. I wasn't a street kid like Quan, but I knew about Merchansin Road. "The Merc hurts" was a slogan but it was true. Everybody knew that, especially Quan.

The further you drove down the Merc, where the side-streets started to have numbers instead of street names, that's where the Merc started to hurt the most. That's where Quan lived. He used to talk about the doors at the detention center as if they were the barred doors of his home. "Gail's gate" was what he called them. Because it became so dangerous at night, the locks came down as soon as the sun did. This made being locked down in Juvi easier for Quan. But

Quan's mom begun working nights so Gail's gate didn't automatically lock at night unless Quan locked it himself. New freedom and new shoes let Quan think all things were new.

I doubt the guy who took them even knew what shoe size Quan wore. I doubt he knew what kind of friend Quan was. The last time I saw Mr. Sam, he told me Quan had someone else's blood on him at the end. Before it would've been good enough to hear that Quan didn't give up his shoes easy. But I would give up my whole closet to see him again.

When my release date came up I got a mentor assigned to me also. I hoped it would be Mr. Sam but he quit. When I turned around it was that guy with the deep voice who was talking about lions, cages, and zoo keepers. His name was Solomon Adi. When my mom told him about Quan, I thought he was about to become my therapist too, but he didn't.

"Let's not bring anything from here with us," was all he said when we drove away from the detention center.

"Anything like what?" I asked my mom, "Is he trying to steal the chairs or something?"

"Ask him what he means, Terrell. It's what he's here for," she said. But I wasn't going to ask him anything.

"Is that who I'm supposed to be around all the time? I rather still be locked up!" I whispered to her with no luck.

"Just get in the back seat, Terrell."

The detention center's supervisors didn't care about what I had to say about receiving mentorship, and my mom cared even less. Anyone volunteering to help her troubled son was welcomed to the family.

My first day back at home wasn't how I'd imagined it. I'd imagined hanging out with my friend, Quan, and his mentor, Mr. Sam. But Mr. Sam was gone and my friend Quan was *gone* gone. My mom did try to make the day special. She made a cake and had some new clothes laid out on my bed for me, but it didn't take more than a second to notice what was missing from my room.

"The TV, it's gone," I said while walking out of my room. I was confused but when someone other than my mother thought it was his place to respond, my confusion quickly became frustration.

"It is not just gone, Terrell. It's been replaced with many more opportunities for you to use your time and your mind wisely," said Mr. Solomon.

All I wanted was for him to use his mind and mind his own business. "Mom? What's up?"

"We want the best for you, Terrell. That means getting the best out of you." Mr. Solomon politely told me. But all I wanted to know was why this stranger was answering for my mother. I remembered him from the JDC but he didn't know us and we definitely didn't know him.

"Mom, can we talk somewhere? Alone?"

But even alone she wasn't trying to hear me out. Somebody really convinced her this was the best thing for me.

Walking out from the living room realizing what I was stuck with, I looked through the window and saw the other person I was stuck with.

"Look who's home. You're not lost in all this free open space, are you?" my sister, Patrice, said.

"It reminds me of the useless space between your ears," I said. It was enough to get her off my back but I knew it wasn't true. It seemed like every brain cell she didn't use getting on my nerves, she used in class. That was the "best out of me" part Mr. Solomon thought he could bring out of me. For a long time, I thought that trash talking kid in the JDC was the best me that I could be, it wasn't. It just took me a while to see that. It also took me awhile to see that learning my place in the family would show me what my place in this world could be. Both places included needing to help my mother more.

"You don't need another job, Denise," my Aunt Yvette told my mother. "When you're not at work you're in school, and when you're not in school, you're taking care of Patrice and Terrell. Where do you see time for another job?"

"I see bills, Yvette, and lots of them. With nobody around here to help me pay them."

But Solomon saw something, too. After looking at the shed in our back yard from the kitchen window for a while, he went outside. Then, I heard his car start and pull out of the parking lot. That was quick, I said to myself. I thought he would at least last the summer. But after my mom went to night school and my aunt went home, I saw his car coming back up the driveway. He was still technically a stranger, so I didn't have to answer the doorbell; but I'm glad I did. He gave me a list of nearby houses and a box of trash bags.

"I saw the way you looked when your mother was considering taking another job. I spoke to all the residents of those homes. The money you will make raking their yards won't solve all your mother's financial problems, but she won't feel alone anymore." That seemed like the longest three hours of my life. After the first two yards, Mr. Solomon rolled his sleeves up and gave me a hand. He didn't help out like I thought he was going to do. He just rolled up his sleeves and started clapping.

"Is this making you happy?" I asked.

"Very happy, yes. A month ago, you were raking trash for nothing. Now you're raking leaves for your family."

I made over two-hundred dollars. I had never even seen two

15

hundred dollars, and before I could even thank the people that paid me, I was already thinking of ways to spend it. It was like Mr. Solomon was reading my mind during the walk home.

"I remember hearing you and your friends discussing shoes, clothes and other things you would purchase if you could. You have some options in your pockets."

"My mom is talking about getting a second job, remember? What other options do I have?"

Mr. Solomon didn't respond. He walked beside me the rest of the way home. I was expecting a good job or something but he just got in his car and drove away. I wanted as many people around as possible when I gave my mom the two hundred dollars. It wasn't every day I put something good in her hands and I wanted a house full of witnesses; but it was just me and her. That turned out to be the only audience I needed. The only time I've seen her cry before then was when my grandmother died. I understood those tears; these tears I didn't.

"Keep it Terrell, just keep it! I'm not doing this again. I just can't!" she screamed.

"Ma, what are you doing? I'm just trying to help."

"With drug money? You think you can help this family with drug money? Like your brother?"

"No, Ma! I ain't selling no drugs! I was raking those folks' yards all day. That's what I was doing. Solomon made it happen for me—for us."

"What?"

"He went around asking people if I could rake their yards for money. They said yes so I did. Why I gotta be a drug dealer?"

Just as I wasn't used to doing something as good as helping my mom, she wasn't used to seeing honest money being made that wasn't being made by her. She didn't apologize for how she reacted but I could tell she was proud of me; she just didn't have much practice at it. I kept raking yards for a while but I didn't earn anything near two hundred dollars again. She ended up getting that second job anyway, and taking a break from school.

While my mom's break from school was just beginning, mine was almost over. I wasn't looking forward to it, or the expectations that came with it.

"You best make it worth it, boy," my aunt said to me the day after mom quit school. "Your mother having to put the brakes on her own education means you better press the gas all the way down on yours. No more taking everything for granted. You're the man of this house now, Terrell."

"I'm thirteen, Aunt Debra," I responded. But I should've known better than that.

"You don't eat like a kid, so don't act like one. Listen to me, Terrell. Despite what you did before, people see a lot of promise in you. Your mother, me and your other aunt, even your new mentor. We all see it. It's your responsibility to prove us all right."

Around the time Aunt Debra had finished talking to me, Mr. Solomon walked into the house. He was very perceptive.

"What are you carrying, Terrell, and why do you look like you don't want it?" he asked.

"What do you mean? I'm just holding the remote control. I'm not carrying anything," I said.

"I'm talking about what your aunt just gave you. I'm talking about responsibility. It only falls where there's room. If your shoulders couldn't bear the weight, it wouldn't be given to you," he said.

"How did you know what she was talking about?" I asked but he didn't answer while my aunt was still there. Mr. Solomon liked to wait until we were alone so we could have "man-time." Another way to force his insight upon me. The more I rejected it, the more he gave it.

"Take pride in what you can shoulder; it won't always be easy but it's yours to carry."

"It's mine to carry because I'm the only target. I'm the only guy around. And stop it with me shouldering stuff. Aunt Debra was just talking about making sure I finish high school—no big deal."

"You're carrying more than you know," he kept saying. "You're carrying a legacy . . ." And so he began to sound like everyone else.

Every black kid was carrying the torch for every Civil Rights marcher who crossed whoever's bridge or refused to get off whoever's bus. It got so old and it didn't stop Mr. Solomon, not even when he crossed a line I didn't want crossed.

"You say you're the only target, but you weren't always the only young man here."

"What?"

"There's an empty room—somebody's not here anymore."

I knew my mom and the JDC superintendent had a meeting with Mr. Solomon about our family but there were things I knew she wouldn't tell them. I didn't think she would talk about Malik.

"That other room doesn't have anything to do with you, Mr. Solomon." My family was none of his business.

My disrespect didn't turn his face inside out like it did the teachers or attendants at the JDC. Not even an "I don't know why I bother" look like my mom sometimes gave. Mr. Solomon looked like he was on my side. It was like he heard something different than what I said. That was the night everything changed. Mr. Solomon had an old, heavy voice like the guy who plays Eddie Murphy's dad on Coming to America but when he left our house that night, an even older voice followed me into the bathroom. I paused as soon as I heard it.

It was an old woman. At first I thought I was imagining things because what she said went along with what Mr. Solomon was saying. But before I would hear anything more, the loudest voice in the neighborhood needed to be heard.

"Terrell!" My sister, Patrice yelled. "Stop stealing my toothpaste!"

"I don't have your toothpaste! Use some nail polish remover; it should work better for you."

I wasn't being honest. I did have her toothpaste; I just wanted to get on her nerves a little. But getting on Patrice's nerves caused me to get toothpaste all over my new shirt. While washing the stain out in the sink, I noticed how it felt to have a bathroom to myself again. Community bathrooms in Juvi took some getting used to. My sister continued yelling and knocking at the door but that bathroom felt larger than any room I've been in a long time—I wasn't in a rush to get out.

I started thinking about how we used to crowd the mirror and flex our muscles after all the push-up contests. So with my shirt already off and my aggravating sister safely on the other side of the door, I started flexing my muscles. The more she yelled, the longer I stayed in the mirror. I guess it was my own way of flexing my muscles at her and her accomplishments at school. That didn't last much longer. My mother's policeman style knock ended my bodybuilding display but before I could pull my shirt back over my head, a face other than mine was staring at me in the mirror.

It was an older lady, the same one whose voice I thought I'd imagined hearing a few minutes earlier. But this time I knew I wasn't imagining things because I could hear my mom from the other side of the door.

"It's not the load that breaks you down, it's the way you carry it" she said. It was the same thing she'd been saying. But that time I saw her. In the bathroom mirror, she was there plain as day.

"Boy, what are you doing in there? Open the door! Terrell!"

By then, I was freaking out; that's what I was doing. In Juvi, if you say you're hearing voices they give you a little doctor's slip. If you say you're seeing faces, they might've given you a straightjacket. Between the old woman I didn't know in the mirror and the angry woman I did know outside that bathroom door, I didn't know who to be more afraid of.

"Boy, the water is not even running, so I know you're just wasting time in there. Tomorrow's your first day of school. Hiding in the bathroom isn't going to make it any less embarrassing. Now, come on out of there."

Being embarrassed about spending my freshman year of high school in juvi was the last thing on my mind. I wanted to know who that woman was. When I finally opened the door, my sister grabbed her toothpaste before she could even see the odd look on my face. My mom saw it, but she didn't know what was behind it.

"Don't worry about how people are going to look at you," she said. "Don't worry about what they're going to say either. You just need to worry about what will happen if you mess up again." It was always like that with her. Always like I was looking for an excuse to fail when I wasn't. I never thought I would actually want to talk to Solomon, but then I did. My mom wasn't trying to hear anything from me but "yes ma'am." I was happy to see Solomon's phone number on the refrigerator.

Right away he said, "only strong shoulders can carry heavy challenges, Terrell. The weight of those challenges might hurt but they won't break you. Not if you walk tall and upright. Stay upright tomorrow, Terrell." He hung up before I could ask how he knew what the woman said or even who she was. That night was the strangest night that I could remember, but it was only the beginning.

CHAPTER TWO

"My ultimate responsibility is to myself..."
—Arthur Ashe

A S A SOPHOMORE returning to gen-pop (general population) was like getting released from real prison. Everyone was asking what it was like on the inside. Probably the most attention you'll ever get, at least that's what I thought. The girls made it easy to think that way, especially the ones in ISS. Whatever someone did to deserve In School Suspension (ISS), the Juvi-crew made them look like rookie delinquents. Lucky for us, no one wanted to stay rookies forever.

Pretty soon everyone in ISS wanted to step up their game to the Juvi level. They started smoking inside of buildings, people who were cutting class started skipping entire days of school, and the girls with dress code violations started coming to school nearly naked. Yeah, I thought it was heaven until I met Mr. Hail.

Mr. Elliot Hail was our new assistant principal. We thought he was the new strength training coach by how his arms looked liked a football players' thighs and the way his Under Armor shirts fit more like underwear. That's a joke we were all careful to keep to ourselves. Mr. Hail didn't play around like some of the teachers. He preached respect and dignity every day, all day. Before becoming our assistant principal, Mr. Hail was a recreational program manager at one of the detention centers in Richmond. Early on he showed how much rules meant to him. "I see your cell phone, Justin! No point in trying to hide now." he said.

My friend Justin lost his phone to Mr. Hail almost every day. They should've been on a family plan as much as they passed Justin's phone back and forth but not me. I was quick to put mine away before anyone saw it, but a little too quick that day. Hearing your new phone drop on the hard hallway floor is the worst sound in the world. And before that crashing sound could get out of my head, it was replaced with a more frightening sound.

"I have always tried to be true to myself, to pick those battles I felt were important. My ultimate responsibility is to myself. I could never be anything else."—Arthur Ashe

The voice sounded like it came over the intercom. I paused to see everyone else's reaction to it but no one reacted. After looking around I looked down at my phone and there it was again, somebody else's reflection staring at me. First an old lady in my bathroom mirror and now some dude with glasses and a tennis racket on my phone. I don't even play tennis, I thought.

He was talking about being "true" to himself and "picking battles he thought were important." I didn't know who he was and I definitely didn't know why he was talking me about being real. I was always real to myself and I wasn't picking any battles. I was just trying to hide my phone from Mr. Hail. As for my "ultimate responsibility" being to myself, well, it was my cell phone. So ultimately, I was trying to hang on to it.

After stuffing my phone into my bag, it was my turn to dodge Mr. Hail on the way to homeroom. Usually, it was easy to know when he was nearby. Whispers of "OH HELL" were passed down the hallways like sticks of chewing gum every time he was spotted. Besides the hallways and cafeteria, most students had no reason to see Mr. Hail. But the ISS regulars had permanent seats outside his office. That's where we would go to get handed our ISS slips and find out how much time we had serve.

The teachers hated when we talked about ISS like it was jail or Juvi. But we needed it to sound like it was more than it really was—that made it marketable. We were stupid enough to think it made us marketable. Plus, we hardly saw real teachers anyway. Those substitutes teaching in ISS weren't real, they didn't even teach. They just wanted the room quiet enough not to interrupt their IPhone movie of the week. But whispering was our thing. We were pros at it. We came up with so many silent schemes in ISS we renamed it "In Secret Society."

"Quiet! This isn't your new hangout spot. It's not the block either. You all couldn't do things the right way in class, so don't think you get to do it your way here!" Mr. Gamble yelled. He was the worst ISS sub we had. We just knew he hated us.

"Maybe if you would spend less time whispering and more time listening, you all wouldn't be in here," he said.

Usually no one was crazy enough to respond to him but Justin always had something to say.

"Have you read the school rule book, Mr. Gamble? Almost anything we do can put us in here," Justin said.

"You're not in here for *almost* doing something, Justin. You're here for advertising your underwear to the entire school."

"I wasn't trying to sag my pants; I just forgot my belt at home was all."

"How many times have you been in here for the same reason, Justin?"

"What can I say; I have a bad memory."

"Or you're just a bad liar? Or maybe you should stop making excuses for yourself. When you graduate, I mean if you ever graduate, no one outside of these school doors will care about your excuses. That goes for any of you. The people who don't care about you are ones out there waiting on you. See if they care if you have a 'bad memory.'"

While Justin was going back and forth with Mr. Gamble, I started thinking about what the guy whose face appeared on my phone said about picking those battles he felt were important. Then I started thinking about why Justin was battling over a rule about sagging pants, something most of us boys loved to do.

"Swag isn't swag if your pants don't sag," Justin said. That got everyone in ISS laughing but it got me thinking. I looked towards the front of the room where Mr. Gamble was sitting. He wore my mother's expression of disappointment as he looked at everyone laughing in agreement with Justin.

But what Justin said was true; at least that's how most of us felt about it. The older boys made it looked good and the girls definitely showed their appreciation. We could almost tell what guys had girlfriends by their obedience to the rules. In a school with rules and dress codes like ours, sagging made us different. When you looked different, girls treated you different. If I thought about the things we did that *wasn't* about getting some girl's attention, the list would be very short.

But no matter how much fun we were having in ISS, it didn't last forever. The school bell always rang, signaling the end of the only part of my day that made sense. It was the only time I was around people I had things in common with. My mom called it being "institutionalized." I was "afraid of being normal" was how she explained it sometimes when I walked into the front door looking like I was walking into a jail cell. Going home for me wasn't like going home for everyone else. Most of my friends didn't know how bad they were. They didn't have reminders in the form of scholarship siblings like me—-lucky for them..

"What are you working towards this week, Terrell? ISS perfect attendance or are you going all the way and get expelled again?"

Patrice thought comments like those were funny. Making the honors society automatically made her a licensed comedian, I guessed. And she was only the first reminder. Everyone that came through our front door has some kind of school success story to remind me of.

Especially my aunt Debra who just earned her Masters of Arts degree in something. Luckily for me, I had already mastered the art of not caring. And I flashed that degree every time one of them tried giving me the third degree.

My sister, mom, aunts, none of them got it. It was like we spoke different languages. They didn't understand I had more going on than what those teachers were talking about. My sister's boyfriend, Shawn, he got it. The way he walked around, the way he dressed, I could tell he understood it. Shawn wasn't wasting time on algebra and history. He was making history. Everyone knew who he was. On the football field, he was already a legend. The crowds were yelling his name more than the name of the team. And the girls—crazy! I thought Shawn dated my sister just to have his own personal tutor. I couldn't see any other reason for him to torture himself. But when my mom and aunts convinced (forced) Shawn to stay for dinner one night, the torture was all mine.

"Do you know what it takes to have a reputation like Shawn's, Terrell?" Aunt Vicky asked.

"Don't just shrug your shoulders, Terrell. You need to start paying attention to young men who are taking life seriously," my mom said while seeing how I perfectly ignored my aunt Vicky. "Time isn't waiting on you; she's waiting to pass by you if you don't start taking her more seriously."

"Her who?" I asked

"Time, boy! What else are we talking about?"

I couldn't tell what my mom was talking at all. She sounded like one of her self-improvement videos. For every comic book or car magazine I was able to sneak into the house, there were five self-help books. If someone owned a business or a church, my mom owned their book. But some of them did come in handy.

When we ran out of paper towels, the sheets from some of her magazines were large enough for a sandwich and some potato chips to fit on. But soon, even the magazine paper wouldn't let me snack in peace.

CHAPTER THREE

". . . for tomorrow belongs to those who prepare for it today."
—Malcolm X

THE WEEKEND CAME and my mom was shopping,my sister was off boring her boyfriend to death, and I was finally going to have the TV remote in my hand and no nagging voice in my ear, at least I thought I was.

"Education is the passport to the future, for tomorrow belongs to those who prepare for it today."

If it wasn't a man's voice, I would've thought my mom snuck into my head. But it wasn't her.

"Tomorrow belongs to those who prepare for it today," He repeated.

At that point my tomorrow was a long boring day at church and an afternoon talking with Solomon.

As far as being "prepared" for it, Solomon would make sure it belonged to me whether I prepared for it or not. So, I didn't see the reason for someone's voice to cut into my snack and TV time. It wasn't every day I had the TV to myself, and WWF Smack Down needed my full attention. Tomorrow will be just another tomorrow, I thought. I started thinking differently when I ran out of BBQ potato chips and noticed what they were hiding. The sheets of my mom's magazine were greasy at that point but the words were still clear.

"Learning what is necessary for tomorrow is the only way to be ready for tomorrow. Tomorrow is the friend and enemy who never postpones his arrival, but greets the prepared and unprepared alike. If you find him first, he will not be found at the end of wide road holding the gates to the future open, but at a secret door reserved for those who've earned a ticket for entry."

After reading that torn sheet of magazine paper and thinking about what that voice said about "who tomorrow belongs to", I knew I hadn't earned my passport to the future. I hadn't even applied for it.

"I don't want to be stuck in yesterday," was the first thing I said when Mr. Solomon showed up that day.

"You don't?" he replied.

"Na, I don't. If there's something better in front of me, I want it."

"Well it's not too late to earn it," he said before looking at the torn magazine page I placed on the counter.

"These words meant something to you?" he asked.

"Yeah, I guess they did."

"What about the words you heard before you read this? What did they mean to you?"

There it was again. He knew! He knew what I'd been hearing. Either I wasn't crazy or we both were. But he wouldn't tell me how he knew. He only explained the messages and the messenger to me.

"He was the very definition of manhood," Mr. Solomon said.

"Why haven't I heard of him?"

"Because he was seen as an extremist, a racist, and a criminal, Terrell." That didn't make any sense, I thought. Why would the voice of a criminal advise me to take my education more seriously? But I kept listening.

"He was seen as an extremist and racist only because he extremely loved his race," Mr. Solomon said with a rare smile on his face. "And just as a judge once indicted and condemned you for your actions against society, this man indicted and condemned society for its actions against his race, our race."

"That made him an extremist?" I asked

"Well let's just say he condemned them in an extreme way, Terrell." Then Mr. Solomon smiled again.

"But passion can easily become extreme. One of the first governors of this great state once yelled 'give me liberty or give me death.' To those he was fighting against, his beliefs were also extreme and criminal."

"Patrick Henry? We learned about him. But what was so criminal about the other man you're talking about? Was he like some of us? Stealing, drugs . . . all that?"

Mr. Solomon was happy to see I even knew who Patrick Henry was. And he answered me quickly.

"Yes, Terrell, all of that. But I'll tell you what his biggest crime was, it was refusing to remain a criminal. He refused to let the six years he spent in prison imprison his mind. His biggest crime was refusing to stay ignorant and uneducated. It was refusing to allow the racially motivated death of his father and other brutalities to turn him into an animal. Instead, he became man. An educated man is more powerful than any beast."

I still didn't know who this man was but Mr. Solomon got excited just talking about him. His eyes lit up like my grandfather's did while talking about the older ball players of his time during the NBA playoffs. But Solomon wasn't interested in talking to me about games. He was on the topic that meant the most to him—prisons.

"Cages are meant to turn men into animals, Terrell." "People do what they have to in order to survive."

"Surviving shouldn't be on your to do list. You were given a mind; minds are meant to thrive. Animals are given claws and fur for the purpose of surviving, not you and I.

I knew what Mr. Solomon meant by cages turning people into animals. Juvi wasn't exactly a prison and some of the guys in there weren't as tough as they pretended to be. Some of them had just followed the wrong crowd and got caught, like my friend Jamal Chambers, Jamal "Chimney" Chambers because of how much marijuana he smoked. That was his thing. He would cut class, miss football practice or even ditch the whole school day to smoke weed. First his teachers, then his coaches started checking behind him—especially his coaches.

Jamal was huge. He was a freshman, but with his football pads on, they said he looked like a varsity player. But Jamal didn't care one way or the other. He didn't like football like that. He didn't like running, hitting, or any of it. So, he showed up less and less to practice then stopped going altogether. Eventually, somebody got with the vice principal of Jamal's high school and checked his wall locker for drugs. They probably could've just asked Jamal to open it. He was that nonchalant about it.

Even with all that, I thought they were wrong putting Jamal in juvi around a bunch of other guys that weren't so nonchalant. Every chance they got, they tested Jamal. Fights, threats, and sometimes they'd mess with his food just because they could. They rode Jamal for being big and soft until he wasn't soft anymore. He became big, mad, and furious all the time. The JDC had to replace a lot of broken tables because of how angry they made Jamal. When Jamal finally got released, it wasn't long before we heard the guards talking about how he was sent to a regular jail after what he did next. None of us were choir boys, but Jamal didn't learn to throw punches until after being used as a punching bag.

Mr. Solomon hated that. I could see it in Juvi and while he was talking about the man he admired so much. But this man made it out.

"Some say his religion set him free; some say it was his anger. I believed his eyes were opened to what he was up against and he wanted to prepare others for what they will be up against. What are you up against, Terrell?"

"Me? Why does everything always have to have something to do with me?"

"You wouldn't have heard his voice unless it was about you. So, tell me, what are you up against?"

I could have given Mr. Solomon a whole list of teachers, school rules, and laws that seemed to had been written just to trip me up but by then I knew that wasn't what he was asking for. I didn't have an answer. Nobody had ever asked me to name my obstacles before. He could see that, so he started naming his. He started talking about moving from Africa to the United States as a teenager in the 1950s. His English was so bad even Black people wouldn't talk to him for long periods of time. After living on the street for a while, he finally got a job in a New York City train station.

That's where he saw two types of African Americans—the ones that knew what a mess they were in and the ones that covered their mess up with fancy suits and dresses. Mr. Solomon didn't see a need to pay malls and clothing stores to hide his circumstances. He said he even tried convincing some of the other low paid workers to save their money but getting ready for Friday nights were as far as some could see, he said. I guess our vision hadn't improved all that much. In Juvi, we laughed about wearing new clothes over old underwear; it started making sense now.

Mr. Solomon admitted to not liking America a lot a first. But one day, years before I heard his voice, Mr. Solomon heard the same voice speaking on the sidewalk near the building he was living in. He had never heard an American speak like that before. It wasn't street talk or slang or anything. He said the man wasn't trying to sell anything, except us to us. The man was trying to sell blackness back to black people. Hearing his words made Mr. Solomon feel better about being black in this country. I guess it made it easier for him to hear the guys on the corners and train stations laugh at his old clothes, deep African accent, and nappy hair. Because Mr. Solomon knew he was the brand of Black that man was selling, not the brand those corner guys were pretending to be.

At the time, he wouldn't tell me who this man was he saw speaking

31

on the sidewalk. Even though, it was the same man speaking to me. He would only say I reminded him of this man.

"Now about that passport to the future; what do you want to do about it?" He asked me.

"I need to apply for one, right?

"What does that mean?" he asked. I hated those kinds of questions. It felt like school had already started.

"I mean, you know, I wanna do better. Patrice be in them college prep classes. I know they got room for me."

"I believe you mean to say, 'I *want* to do better' and 'Patrice is taking *those* college prep classes."

In my head I said "whatever" in the most R rated way I could think of. But on the outside I just nodded my head while Mr. Solomon kept talking.

"But as for those college prep courses, I believe you have to earn your way into those. Or earn your ticket as your mother's magazine said. Which leads us to the issue; how do we earn that ticket?"

"I gotta, I mean, I need to do better in the classes I'm taking now, I guess."

"That is correct."

So that's what I did. I started speaking proper English in English class and running my mouth in history class became a thing of history; but no one seemed to notice, not even the teachers. But the other students, they definitely noticed.

CHAPTER FOUR

"I Was A Stranger In A Strange Land."

—*Harriet Tubman*

WHAT'S UP, TERRELL? What's with those khakis? You're looking like you're trying out for the chess club," Phillip, one of the upperclassmen said.

"Na man, I'm just tired of being sent to ISS every other day."

"But not too tired to study. You're not even stuck in our remedial reading classes anymore."

"That's because I'm not remedial," I said. I probably should've said it in different way by the way Philip started walking towards me. "I'm saying none of us are remedial, Phillip. I decided to show it is all."

"You're showing something alright," he said while stepping back. "But don't show up around the way again until I recognize you again."

Around the way meant his house. Philip lived close the park where we all played basketball so we sometimes got off the bus there. Playing until the street lights came on was our favorite thing to do. But being more committed to class made them less committed to me. Looking down at my pants that for the first time weren't hanging off my behind made me laugh. It was sad and funny at the same time. The teachers always said "don't get caught with your pants down" but it felt worse getting caught with my pants up.

"Later losers," one of them said while jumping from the bus to the basketball courts. From the windows I watched as they divvied the teams before we pulled off. Seemed like I watched from the windows for the rest of my sophomore year. Everyone and everything I used to be a part of was on the other side of some kind of glass. Bus windows, car windows, classroom windows, and fun were all around me and all I could do was window shop.

When my sophomore year was almost over, the Senior Prom and underclassman dances were all everyone could talk about. It was the worst time to be a window shopper. To keep the male and female ratio even, the school didn't allow anyone to come alone. That counted me out big time. My house wasn't close to the school but it felt like it was. I could hear every song and see every girl I wanted to dance with. Even if it was only in my head, I could hear all the fun they were having.

I must've checked my phone a thousand times that night. No vibrations, noise, blinking lights, nothing. Suddenly I was the new kid with no friends. That's when I heard her.

"I had crossed the line. I was free; but there was no one to welcome me to the land of freedom. I was a stranger in a strange land."

A stranger in a strange land was exactly how I felt. But the rest of it didn't make sense, at least not yet.

I remained a "stranger" for most of that summer. Without hearing from my friends, the only noise I could depend on was the sound of Mr. Solomon's car struggling to get up our driveway to take me to some African American history site. That summer, before my junior year, he convinced my mom to let him take me down to the slave museum in Charleston, South Carolina. It was the last place I wanted to go.

As soon as we got out the car, I started sweating. It was the hottest place on earth, but what I would soon see was chilling, even in that weather—a pair of rusty shackles laying on a display table.

"These were chosen for us, Terrell. And now we choose our own," Mr. Solomon said.

He saw the look on my face. By that time Mr. Solomon was used to my confused expressions.

"What were these things used for?" He asked me.

"I don't know. To keep slaves controlled, I guess." I said.

"Did you feel controlled in the detention center? Did you even feel controlled in In School Suspension?"

"Not really," I said. "I just felt like I had to wait my time out."

"Yes, waiting the time out is one way of seeing it. These shackles were used to wait generations out, Terrell. Who can possibly know what those enslaved generations could have meant to their world? Who can know what this enslaved generation could still mean to this world?"

While Solomon was talking, I saw people react differently than when he was talking to us in the detention center. Nobody was smirking, walking away, or even shaking their heads. They just listened. Even the people who were taking pictures and buying souvenirs listened in.

"Don't let your ability to come and go deceive you. We're not all free of these shackles. You Terrell, your eyes have followed every attractive teenage girl that has passed you by. For whatever length of time, each one of them has owned your attention span. By owning your focus, even for a time, they've owned you. How many masters did you have just today alone?"

I couldn't count how many girls walked by me that day or how many I looked at and I definitely wasn't going to count with all those people looking at us.

"Why are we enslaved so easily? What makes us so different? Surely what's appealing to us is equally appealing to the rest of the world. Yet these common things hold so much power over us. Vehicles, jewelry, the body of the opposite sex. This was our jewelry," he said while picking up a pair of shackles. "By the strength of our legs or backs, we were the vehicles and our women our greatest resource. Their gentle

35

touch and soft voices were the ointment that healed what the masters tore open. Now you young men treat these resources as amusement parks."

"No one is amused. Who taught us this? We surely weren't born this way. Look at them."

When I turned to look at a young group of kids playing with each other while their parents were listening to Mr. Solomon, I saw something I would've never noticed before.

"At what point does that innocent affection become something selfish? Children play together for no purpose but for play. Only offering fun and laughter, and taking nothing away from each other. The girls you lust after, what are you offering them, Terrell? What are you trying to take away?"

Then he picked up another pair of shackles and said, "Enough has been taken away."

The drive home was long and Mr. Solomon's silence made it seem even longer. I kept looking over at him wondering what made him different from everybody else, not just the guys either. The grown women I knew were also wearing shackles. Their shackles were fancy but they were still shackles. My Aunt Debra called it "status."

"Once the titles of your degree go from Associates to Bachelor to Masters, your status increases, too . . ." Aunt Debra had said.

That was a part of a long speech she gave me at the Mercedes dealership before buying her dream car. I thought she brought me there to show me what hard work could accomplish, but I could tell she'd rehearsed that speech the whole way there. When she found out her dream car wouldn't be ready in time for some big concert, that was when my aunt's shackles began to show themselves.

Apparently the music at the concert wouldn't sound the same if she couldn't drive her new car there. My mom and Aunt Debra argued for a week over missing the concert. I didn't call it "shackles" then but I knew there needed to be a name for it. But there were no shackles on Mr. Solomon. His shoes weren't made by anyone important; his watch was his only jewelry and with the shape his car was in, he spent more money on gas than he ever did on a car payment.

I thought about the woman's words again.

"I had crossed the line. I was free; but there was no one to welcome me to the land of freedom. I was a stranger in a strange land."

Mr. Solomon was the stranger I began to think. He didn't fit in this place. And the reason why there was no one to welcome him was because he wasn't trying to fit in. He was talking about shackles, chains, and baby mamas as if he was looking down on us. The car stayed quiet the rest of the ride home until we got to my driveway.

"Who are 'us?'" he asked.

"What?"

"Us, you said I'm looking down on 'us.' But I only see you here. Who do you represent?"

Suddenly things got as strange as they did when I first saw that woman's reflection in my bathroom mirror.

"I'm not a mind reader, Terrell. I only hear what you say. Now hear what I'm asking. Who do you represent?"

"I represent people, people my age back home."

"So tell me about people your age back home."

"What?"

"We have over an hour left to drive, Terrell. Let me hear about your ambassadorship."

"My what?"

"Ambassadors represent the principles of their people, Terrell. Tell me about yours."

The last hour of that drive felt like an eternity. I talked about sports and technology and anything else I saw that people my age are into. But Mr. Solomon saw it differently.

"I don't see the young people in your community contributing much technology, Terrell. I see them contributing their money to technological manufacturers. Then I see how so many of you use this technology to gain access to each other and exploit each other."

"You mean social media?"

"I mean requesting dangerous pictures and videos from each other, suggestive pictures, Terrell. Don't pretend to not know what I'm talking about."

"They're pictures, Mr. Solomon. Not weapons of mass destruction."

"Aren't they, Terrell? When you break a young girl's trust and share these photos with others, a massive amount of destruction is done to every girl involved. Other than this sort of shame and the continued production of single mothers, what is it your people are doing, Terrell—as their ambassador?

"Well, I'm obviously not contributing to the amount of baby mamas. You can't put that on me."

"Every young woman you gaze upon is more likely to be your baby's mother instead of a wife, Terrell. Do you have any interest in marrying all these girls? Of course not. If you find yourself "getting lucky" enough to be unlucky, you and that unlucky girl could easily add to this horrible statistic."

"Why is it always on us, the guys? You always make it about what men do as if girls do not make their own choices."

"Are you a leader or not? When wives were a young man's first and most noble pursuit, young girls grew up wanting to be wives. Now that's no longer the case. Yet, young women still want to become mothers at some point, like your mother and your aunt Debra. Mothering wasn't meant to come first."

I hated defending my generation to Mr. Solomon, especially when I couldn't think of a good defense. All I could think of was how many times I heard girls on the school bus or in the cafeteria call some rapper or singer their future "baby's daddy." Hearing all of that seemed stupid but with 72 percent of us (African Americans) only having one parent at home, I guess if they assumed they would be single moms one day, it was better to pick a famous baby daddy. At least that's what I thought. But Mr. Solomon's point became clearer.

People expected the norm and becoming somebody's baby's mama was normal to them. It was all they saw, and not only with younger women.

I didn't know what a biological clock was, but my mom said Aunt Debra's was "ticking like a time bomb"; and waiting around for a husband was like waiting around for the bomb squad. And who wants to wait for that?" By the ratio of married and unmarried parents I knew, looked like nobody wanted to wait. Aunt Debra spent years just waiting for her boyfriend, Kenny, to "grow up and pull his pants up" as my mom often put it. Kenny was cool. He was like an older version of Malik, and my aunt hated that.

"Pull your pants up! If you can't have a degree by your name, at least you can have a belt on your waist. If I can't have a man who is successful, at least he can successfully keep his clothes on," Aunt Debra said at her baby shower.

She never came out and said it, not around me at least; but I always knew she was ashamed of her boyfriend. Having a baby on the way, no wedding ring on her finger, and no husband, I think it made her ashamed of herself too. She and my mom talked so much about standards and there she was with Kenny; but he didn't care.

"I didn't need a belt or degree to successfully put a baby in your belly, so get on with opening your gifts. The game is about to come on."

Everyone was eating my mom's red velvet cupcakes when we heard it, but I was the only one able to swallow. All the women in my aunt's living room just sat there staring at Ken with their mouth's full of cheesecake frosting. It was almost like swallowing the cupcake would mean digesting Kenny's comeback. Needless to say after that, Kenny never came back.

Only the woman's words came back. I was still hearing the loud sounds of Mr. Solomon's muffler but her words were clear.

"I had crossed the line. I was free; but there was no one to welcome me to the land of freedom. I was a stranger in a strange land."

That time it made more sense to me, once I applied it to what I knew. I knew the woman was talking about crossing over to a side she hadn't been before and becoming a stranger in an environment she hadn't been before. My aunt wanted to believe success placed her into that new environment, but it hadn't. Mentally, she hadn't crossed any lines. Her attitude about her car, about success, and even Kenny were all examples of that; and they later became examples to me.

But as I was sitting there thinking about my aunt and her infamous baby shower, Mr. Solomon was still waiting on an answer to his question. I held to my guns and I did the best I could at the time.

"Things happen, Mr. Solomon. When people are having fun or doing whatever, nobody wants to think about consequences. Outside of technology, my generation isn't all that different than my mom's. You make it seem like there's something wrong with us but we're just having fun and it's been like this before us."

Although those "guns" were more like water pistols, I wanted to put up some kind of defense.

"Terrell, do you remember the first time I came over for dinner? Your Aunt Debra made her lasagna."

"Yes, it was horrible. So what?"

"It was horrible. But your aunt wasn't horrible. Neither were the hands or pots and pans she was using."

"I'm lost, Mr. Solomon."

"The recipe was the problem. There was nothing wrong with your aunt just like there is nothing wrong with any of us. After she changed her recipe, none of us could've had enough of her lasagna. What of the recipe of men, Terrell? Have we had enough of that yet, as nasty as it's proven to be? Or do we just leave it on the menu and say the choice is theirs?"

CHAPTER FIVE

"From what we get, we can make a living;
what we give, however, makes a life."

—*Arthur Ashe*

A FTER THAT TALK about the ingredients of men and lasagna we went inside my house where my mom saved us some spaghetti. That wasn't all she left on the table for me. I wasn't sure it was for behaving or no longer complaining about spending my entire summer with Mr. Solomon, but my mom did it big with my school clothes that summer.

All the top name brand gear was on that table and I couldn't wait to show it off. I started matching up jeans with shirts and t-shirts with shorts, but while I was adding, Mr. Solomon was behind me subtracting—subtracting how much my mom sacrificed to put that smile on my face. That was something Mr. Solomon was good at,

"If your smiles aren't at least equally shared by the ones who made you smile, you should be ashamed of being happy," was how he explained it.

He was the ultimate buzz-killer. But I didn't make it easy for him to kill mine. Even though I knew about my mom's money situation, I also knew how serious and responsible she was. I thought that was why she didn't have time to get as excited as I did. But the more I looked at those price tags, the more my excitement fizzled. It was like receiving cheers for scoring the game winning touchdown and forgetting all my team did to put me in scoring position. For me to score style points at school, team-mom had to stretch her money a lot more than she should have to.

But that wasn't what Mr. Solomon was shaking his head about. He wasn't as concerned about what my mom was willing to buy me as much as he was concerned about those things I thought I needed. I didn't think Mr. Solomon knew how it felt to pull the tag off a new shirt or the paper stuffing out of a new pair of shoes. It made me not care about bills, food, or anything else my mother's money could've been used for. No matter how good her cooking was, I couldn't taste it after it's gone. But those shoes were going to look good again and again.

"You're richer than you know, Terrell. Your mind—it's a money-making machine. But your eyes and your appetite spend before your mind can invest."

"My appetite?" I said, "What does food have to do with anything."

"There are different appetites, Terrell. Consider your need for those shirts with the horseman on them."

"You mean Polo shirts, Mr. Solomon. Ralph Lauren makes popular stuff."

"No, Ralph Lauren makes money, Terrell. The shirts aren't popular until some young man like you says they are in his music video. That's the power of influence. Other teenagers at your school will be watching you, not because of how you look but how you look at things. Terrell is different, they will say. Most will only say it to themselves, but they will still say it and because of who Terrell is, those Polo shirts will become important once Terrell puts them on, not while they're hanging on the racks."

Mr. Solomon went home after saying that. I just stood there thinking why I shouldn't wear name brand stuff. Good grades cost me my friends; I didn't want a good conscience to cost me my clothes, too. That's when I heard,

"From what we get, we can make a living; what we give, however, makes a life."

That was music to my ears. Finally, one of the voices were on my side, I thought. I wished I could've recorded it and played if for Solomon.

"From what we get, we can make a living," must've been talking about my mom and her job, and "what we give, however, makes a life," must've meant giving me the clothes that made my life better. It all made sense to me, but those words were only the beginning of my lesson.

They began to follow me.

"What we give" was echoed throughout my house.

I heard it hanging up my new clothes and while folding my old ones. Even in the kitchen while microwaving mom's spaghetti, *"what we give"* was following me everywhere. It was like we had surround sound all of a sudden. Then suddenly it wasn't sound that I was surrounded by, but visions of much older people from an older time. One old lady was on a farm or in a field or something. Her back was to me but I could tell she was old by her housecoat and the way she hunched over. She turned and whispered, "that's enough weight for this morning child, I reckon you and I better get to your lessons while the gettin is good."

School didn't start for another week. I didn't know what she was talking about or who she was, but she was looking right at me. But it wasn't my response she was waiting for. Behind me was another vision of a much younger child in the same field.

"I'll hurry, mama Agnes and I'll be careful. Mr. Beckwith won't catch any of us."

I didn't know who Mr. Beckwith was but right then I saw a man on a horse galloping right at me. It looked too real to be a vision. What he said to the old lady became too real to be a dream.

"Where are they, Agnes? Where are the children? Every day about this hour this plantation seems to be missing a few Negro children. Let those cotton scales be light, you hear me? Your backs will reap the rewards."

There was a reward the old lady was hoping to reap but it wasn't for herself, and it definitely wasn't lashes from the man's whip. Then she repeated those words I'd been hearing.

"From what we get, we can make a living; what we give, however, makes a life."

Free work was what Mr. Beckwith got from Agnes and the other slaves, which was his *"living."* But education was what she wanted to give to the children of that plantation. She knew that could "make a life" for them. They risked everything to hide their classes because learning was all that mattered, not even food, and definitely not clothes. I realized no one needed nice clothes or even a full stomach to focus in class when they truly believed their futures depended on it. After seeing all of that, I didn't want to be an exception to that rule. As quickly as I hung those clothes up, half of them were back on the table. I wanted to put some of the money back into my mom's purse and take the shame off my shoulders. My mom returned home from work and I was waiting to show her the table full of clothes she could return. But before I could surprise her, we were both surprised when all the lights went out.

"Mom! Where's the flashlight?"

My mom didn't answer me. It was a different voice I heard and the light that shone from the table where my clothes were was no flashlight. It was a man's face. A white man's face.

"Clothes and manners do not make the man; but when he is made, they greatly improve his appearance."—Arthur Ashe

I didn't recognize his voice or his face, and just like that the lights were back on and he was gone.

"But when he is made," the voice repeated.

I started thinking about what he meant by "when he (a man) is made." Then I looked around the corner and saw my mom. She was reaching up above the refrigerator into a little dish we kept coins in.

She counted it then put in her purse. It couldn't have been more than two dollars but I could tell it was an important two dollars. The money I made that summer from cutting grass and raking leaves was hidden in my room. I thought I'd earned it enduring the sun and all those African American history sights Mr. Solomon drug me to. But then I thought about Ms. Agnes and those kids and how they risked their lives to have the opportunities I took for granted. And how my mom put her own education on hold to help me with the second chances I'd been given. The money I hid away began to feel more like a curse than something I was entitled to. Putting it on the table with those new clothes didn't feel great, but it felt right.

The white man whose face shone from our kitchen table was an abolitionist named Henry Ward Beecher. In the 19th century he was one of many white men working to free slaves from their chains. Seeing his face and hearing his voice must've meant I was still wearing mine.

"Clothes and manners do not make the man; but when he is made, they greatly improve his appearance" was what he told me. And he was right.

The clothes I wore and even the manners that Mr. Solomon helped to improve didn't make me the young man my teachers expected me to be. They didn't make me the young man my mom needed me to be either. There was still work to be done. And as the summer leading to my junior year was finishing and the new school year beginning, those voices would have another influence to compete with.

CHAPTER SIX

"Our lives begin to end the day we become silent
about things that matter."

—*Martin Luther King Jr.*

NOTHING SAID THAT the school year had begun like the sound of sports, and that's all I heard on the school bus that first day. Not being an underclassmen anymore must've meant we could talk as loud as we wanted because I thought I was deaf by the time our bus arrived at school. As soon as I got off the bus, and as soon as my hearing came back, I was surprised to hear people calling my name so much.

All the "what's ups" and "where you beens" were different than what I expected, especially with how my sophomore year ended. Before the homeroom bell rang, most of the guys had already started picking their teams for the basketball games we played during gym. Being included again felt good. It felt like it did at the beginning of my sophomore year, before following the rules made me feel invisible. But now that everyone could see me again, they expected the old me. That's what being included meant. That was all it meant. My friend Tawanna Anderson learned this before I did. And seeing her that first day back, wearing makeup and tighter fitting clothes, made me think Tawanna learned some other things, too.

She was a junior like me but, unlike me, Tawanna spent her summer hanging with our friends, Cory and Jaylon. House parties and (marijuana) smoke outs were all they bragged about doing over the summer. Tawanna didn't brag any, but it was obvious she was a part of it. The faraway look in her eyes reminded me of the way my big brother looked the first time he got involved in the things that he regretted. And the more they all talked, the more I realized some things about Tawanna's summer that weren't so obvious.

"We're gonna skip auto shop, right?" said Cory.

"Yeah but we gotta make sure she can meet us behind school," Jaylon responded.

As they kept trying to figure out how to sneak away with some girl, I began thinking about what Mr. Solomon said at that slave museum, about treating young ladies like "amusement parks". I hated thinking that, especially knowing my mom or sister could easily be included in that cycle. When Tawanna started talking, my hate turned to sadness.

"I can just play like I'm sick. They'll let me out of class. It worked every time this summer with my mom, right?

Cory and Jaylon got excited, but I didn't know how to feel. We were all friends. I kept looking at Tawanna but she wouldn't look back at me. She just kept reassuring Cory and Jaylon that their plan would work. It was like she needed them to be comfortable when she obviously wasn't.

Because of the way my grades improved the end of my sophomore year, I wasn't in all of the same classes they were anymore. But after second period when Cory and Jaylon's auto shop class was beginning, it was all I could think about.

We were together again for gym period but Tawanna didn't dress out. She sat on the bleachers and watched us play basketball. Before long, she wasn't watching anymore. Because I'd spent most of the summer alone, nobody knew how much I improved on my ball handling, especially my crossover. But no matter how many guys I shook on the court, no one seemed more shaken than my friend, Tawanna.

"Shoot it or pass it!" one of my teammates yelled.

My mind wasn't on the game anymore, so I passed it. I wanted to pass on all of it. Playing ball, joking around about girls, and I definitely wanted to pass on whatever they did to Tawanna. The only thing that felt right was walking over and sitting next to her but I didn't. I didn't agree with them but I still cared about what they thought. I guess I passed on doing the right thing for my friend, too. Instead, I did the easy thing. Faking an ankle injury and limping off the court took me out the game and out of Tawanna's sight. For the rest of that day my conscience limped more than I ever did.

I got over it. I had to. I saw Tawanna laughing and joking with them in the hallway after school so I thought I felt bad for no reason at all. That also made the bus ride home easier. Joining in on some of the inappropriate conversations made me feel like my old self and less like an outsider. But when the bus stopped at Philip's house (near the outdoor courts), nothing had changed. They all ran by off the bus without even looking back.

When I got off the bus and didn't see Mr. Solomon's car in the driveway, I was glad. There wasn't much homework the first day, so I could watch as much TV as possible. But when I walked inside, I saw my mom was already in the living room watching TV. Even after I was done with my homework, she was still watching TV. Even after going back to double check my work, she was still sitting there.

"Instead of waiting me out, why don't you just come have a seat? I don't have school tonight. I'm taking notes from this documentary instead."

"You're going to nursing school? What does this kind of stuff have to do with being a nurse?" I asked. But I didn't care what my mom was actually watching, I just wanted the remote control.

"You see disturbing things as a nurse, Terrell. Some of the diseases and injuries we treat come from young men and women that find themselves in these kinds of situations."

"What kind of situations?" I asked. Then I looked at what she was watching. It was exactly what I would have been watching, but for very different reasons.

"Mom, you're watching a show about clubs and partying?"

"It's a DVD about the influences that alcohol and drugs have on nonconsensual sex. Do you know what that means?"

"No means no, Ma. I know already."

"It's not just 'no means no.' It's no means no when you're sober, but everything means no when drugs or alcohol is involved. That's what this film is about. Our busiest hours in emergency rooms are after midnight. Where do you think all those patients come from, Terrell?

I didn't care where my mom's patients came from. What I was seeing on the TV looked like somewhere I wanted to be.

"I don't know, Ma. I mean, it's sad people end up in hospitals, but you can't make it seem like all those people don't like doing whatever it is they're doing. Just look at them."

"Just keep your eyes open, Terrell. You will see a lot of people volunteering to do things they really don't want to do."

I tried listening to my mother but she didn't make any sense. None of it made any sense. I didn't know anyone who volunteered for things they didn't want to do. Who would want to, I thought. Then I thought I was hearing something again.

My mom's radio hadn't worked in forever, but I was sure the voice was coming from it. Mom turned and looked towards the kitchen, too. That's when I heard him more clearly.

"Our lives begin to end the day we become silent about things that matter."

"You heard it too, mom? Didn't you?" I yelled. "Your radio!"

Before my mom could reply with "all I heard was my timer on the microwave, so bring me my popcorn," I was already standing over her with her radio in my hands. With the dangling cord distracting her view, she turned and looked at me as if I was losing it. Then I realized the radio was already unplugged when I grabbed it. Maybe I am losing it, I thought. Hearing voices isn't normal. But before I could totally convince myself that I was crazy, my mom pointed my attention towards something on the documentary, a nightclub from our area. I guess it hit the big time to be a part of some research study.

But the name of the club wasn't all my mom recognized. Some of the people being recorded went to school with my brother. I didn't know them but my mom remembered them.

"Those two used to cheer at Malik's basketball games the loudest," she said.

Now I was watching them being led from the club by some guy. They could barely walk on their own, but the guy did all he could to keep them heading towards his car. The video showed a couple of security guards watching, but only watching. Then it showed the guys' tail lights disappearing in the night.

"Just like that," my mom said while shaking her head.

That got me wondering if Tawanna, Cory and Jaylon happened just like that. I didn't think it happened at a club but it could've been anywhere. We were calling Tawanna a light-weight the first time we all smoked pot. Now they call her marijuana-Tawanna. She used to be the only one convincing me to at least try to do my homework. Now I was afraid to think of what she'd been convinced to do.

"Our lives begin to end the day we become silent about things that matter."

That time I heard him, and not just the sound of his voice. I heard every word. I thought about how I punked out on the basketball court by staying quiet about Tawanna.

"Our lives begin to end the day . . ."

I didn't want my life to end, not the part that mattered. The part that acted like my friend didn't matter. Tawanna mattered.

The next day all I wanted to do was tell Tawanna that whatever was going on, didn't have to continue if she didn't want it to. But nothing that day turned out the way I had hoped. My mom was running late for work, so she didn't make breakfast. I was running late for school, so I didn't make the bus and my aunt was running low on patience, so I heard it from her the entire way to school. But while Aunt Debra was scolding me about responsibility, I was still able to hear someone whispering in my ear.

"In all our deeds, the proper value and respect for time determines success or failure."

It was a man's voice, the same man who told me "Education is a passport to the future." But this time, I didn't know what it meant. My aunt was going on about success and failure too but later on I would understand her version of it.

As soon as I walked into school, the first bell for class rang. Homeroom was quiet that day, very quiet. Not a "let's be obedient" kind of quiet, but a "nobody says anything because if we do, we won't stop laughing" kind of quiet. I was left out of the joke—that felt familiar. After the next bell, I saw Cory, Jaylon, and this new guy, Torry, walking down the hall laughing with everyone else; but something didn't look right. Then someone told me what I was looking at.

"Did you get yours, too?" he said.

I knew what that meant, but at the same time, I didn't know what he was specifically talking about.

"Tawanna and Torry, man. You haven't heard?"

I hadn't heard anything, and for a few minutes after he told me, I couldn't hear anything else. I just stood still in silence while everyone continued walking. I could still see Cory and Jaylon, but they were far away by then. They were far away from Tawanna, too.

"In all our deeds, the proper value and respect for time determines success or failure."—Malcolm X.

Those words made sense to me after that. I had an opportunity to do a good thing but I didn't do it. I didn't respect that the time for any good deed is now, not tomorrow. I should not have needed a video to remind me to do the right thing, I should not have needed voices either. Only courage.

CHAPTER SEVEN

"I was a stranger in a strange land."
—Harriet Tubman

"I HAD CROSSED THE line. I was free; but there was no one to welcome me to the land of freedom. I was a stranger in a strange land."

For the next month this was all I could hear, every night. The nights I didn't hear those words, I was up thinking about what they meant. I didn't catch a break at school either. When I thought about my friends doing things without me, I would hear those words again. I couldn't figure them out like before. I tried asking Mr. Solomon but he refused to help.

I didn't expect my teachers to know anything about the voices but I was at least hoping they would notice my improvements in class. Ever since I moved to the front of the class, grades became the only way to stand out.

Progress reports and report cards only came out during select times of the semester, so a few of the teachers would read our exam scores out as if they were statistics from some sporting event. It was ok at first but after a while the nine or ten of us that actually cared soon realized it was only nine or ten of us that actually cared.

"Once our hard work is recognized, the doors of opportunity will swing open," was the motto.

It sounded good but most of the other students weren't willing to keep gambling our high school fun on that, especially when the recognition for the best grades wasn't nearly as loud as the laughter and cheering for someone doing something inappropriate. I couldn't see all this back when I was spending my energy trying to be noticed; being invisible took less effort, and I saw a lot more.

I saw why some students viewed behaving and doing their best in class as the only way to succeed in life. It was like college was in front of them and it was the only thing they could see. The others, like me, we could see everything. We could see college a mile down the road. But parties, the opposite sex, and the other distractions were only a few feet away, inches away. Some of us thought sports was our ticket to college. We practiced dribbling and shooting like it was chemistry and algebra, even though we only knew chemistry and algebra teachers—not professional athletes.

Those were my friends. At least they were before my passport to the future (education) became more important than my hood pass. But it was still hard being right there. I started to hope becoming a better student would change my environment, move me to a different class. It didn't. I had only crossed the street, where I could still look to the other side and see what I was missing out on. That was when those words that were haunting me began to help me.

"I had crossed the line. I was free; but there was no one to welcome me to the land of freedom. I was a stranger in a strange land."

I, too, had crossed a line; and there was no one to welcome me either. Not my friends, because they weren't interested in crossing to the side where following the rules and excelling in class were the most important things. Not even the teachers welcomed me. They were too used to me being on the side that would disrupt class rather than the side that would participate in it. It wasn't a strange land but I felt like a stranger.

I had crossed over to an invisible group of normal students who didn't know me and teachers who weren't sure how long I would be okay with being invisible. But, like I said, invisibility showed me things. It showed me what side of the winning team I was actually on. When I was still sitting in the back of class with my friends, we thought we were winning when we weren't. None of us knew any better. We didn't see any examples of winners being created in school. Our idea of winning came from people who bragged about winning— athletes and entertainers. But we were looking in the wrong places, the faraway places.

Nearby were winners we didn't recognize. I never saw the doctor who prescribed my aunt's medicine around town, but he was from the neighborhood. The owner of the auto shop where my mother got her car repairs took the same auto body class we all used to skip. She never stopped complaining about his prices but she never stopped paying them, either. Even the district attorney who presented my juvenile case. She was arguing against me but not against justice. We didn't recognize these winners; we didn't even recognize the winners who were teaching us every day how to win.

Mr. Wilks knew none of us wanted to be like him, a school teacher. His car wasn't fancy and besides asking us to sit down and be quiet every day, he didn't seem to be the boss of anything. In fact, he was so opposite of what I thought a boss was. Instead of yelling and demanding things, he tried to give us as many choices as possible. "Driving your own bus," was what he called it. And some of us threw him under that bus every chance we got.

Asking for bathroom passes and not returning to class was my usual way. The next day of class I always saw the look of disappointment on his face, but he never had an ISS slip in his hand. Doing the right thing without fear of punishment was what he wanted for us. That was winning to him. That was the side he tried to pull me to. We were playing tug-a-war for my future and every excuse or insult I gave put oil on the hands of every person that tried to help me. Thinking my attitude was putting my teachers in their place caused me to slip further from my rightful place and further from the passport I'd begun to want so much.

That's when I learned that after slipping away for my entire sophomore year, I wasn't able to just slip back.

"A passport to the future is an interesting concept, Terrell. But if you want the responsibility of student class president, show that you can not only follow the rules but encourage others to do so as well. This is a problem with much of society. We seem to think being a good citizen is a solo sport. It's time to encourage the others to be better students also."

"It's been half a year already, Mr. Wilks. Who's been better than me?" I said.

"Slates aren't wiped clean overnight, Terrell. A few trouble-free months isn't something to brag about. Just continue what you're doing, we'll see about the leadership opportunities."

Being picked for class president or even class leader for a short time, was a big deal to all those honor society committees that my sister was a part of. When I told Mr. Wilks about "passport to the future," I didn't really know what the future held; but being a class leader, someone in charge, was what I wanted right then.

"Not now doesn't mean no, Terrell. You should learn and accept the difference. It's a part of growing up."

"I hear you, Mr. Wilks. It's just that . . ." Before I could get my words out, I heard something being whispered in my ear.

"If you're paid before you walk on the court, what's the point in playing as if your life depended on it?"

"Terrell, you were saying something?" Mr. Wilks asked. "Hurry now, the next bell is about to ring."

"It's nothing Mr. Wilks. I understand what you're saying. I'll go to class."

So I went but I didn't get far. Before I got down the hallway that same voice returned saying the same thing.

"If you're paid before you walk on the court, what's the point in playing as if your life depended on it?"

56

It was the voice of that guy who appeared on my phone, the one holding a tennis racket. As I was walking and trying to figure out the meaning of his message, I saw a maintenance man standing on a ladder. I don't know what he was struggling with, but I knew if he could quit and still get paid he would've. But it didn't work like that for him so why should it work like that for me, I thought.

If Mr. Wilks made me the class leader before I've actually earned it, I would not have done my job the way I would've if I really earned it. As soon as I understood that, I wanted to let Mr. Wilks know before he started thinking I was still lazy and unwilling to work for what I wanted. But when I got back to his class, someone was already changing his mind, in a different way.

"You weren't in the teacher's lounge," said Mr. Moyer, one of the other ISS teachers.

"No, Terrell Hayes wanted to talk after class."

"Terrell Hayes? I thought he dropped out of school. What could he want? Was he trying to talk himself out of suspension this time?

"You probably thought he dropped out because he's been staying out of trouble and steering clear of your ISS rooms."

"So he's learned how to pull his pants up and stay off his cell phone?"

"His recent progress report suggests he's learned a lot more than just that. He's been among the best in class since the start of this year.

Last year ended pretty well for him, too. He's been campaigning for class leadership."

"Class Leadership?"

"Yes, so far he's been as good as anyone. I think he has his mind on applying for college prep courses."

"College prep?"

"That's what I said."

"Those classes are to prepare kids for college. We get additional funding to pay for those classes for just that reason."

"What's your point?"

"Terrell Hayes is more likely to be seen walking in a prison lineup than across some college graduation stage. That's my point."

"Well that's awesome John. I'm sure the kids appreciate how much faith their teachers have in them."

"I don't walk by faith, Stewart (Wilks). I walk by sight. And that's what I've been seeing since the Juvenile Detention Center dumped him in our lap."

I knew Mr. Moyer wasn't a big fan of mine, but I thought he would be happy to hear of my improvements. But he didn't seem to be. I walked away thinking about what my mom said before I was sent to Juvie,

"A diploma or a criminal record, one of those will be your first biography, Terrell. You choose what they read about you because it might be *all* they read about you."

Mr. Moyer definitely wasn't interested in reading anything else. And he seemed to have more of an influence on Mr. Wilks than my grades did.

CHAPTER EIGHT

"There is in this world no such force as the force of a person determined to rise,"

—*W. E. B. Du Bois*

THE REST OF that week was quiet. I barely made a sound in or outside of class. By that part of my junior year teachers began to count on me to break the ice during question and answer time, but not anymore. They could thank Mr. Moyer for that and they weren't the only ones noticing that I was less interested in learning.

Mr. Solomon tried trapping me with one of his sermons

"...nobody has ever slid upwards, Terrell. After sliding down a slide, no one's ever slid back up. You spent most of your sophomore year sliding, now you have to climb back. It takes longer, it's slippery, and never easy, but it's the best way."

Mr. Solomon hardly ever saw things my way. I tuned out the first part of his sermon but when he started talking about sliding, it reminded me of the game of tug-a-war I used to play with Mr. Wilks and the other teachers. I had to admit that Mr. Moyer was also on the other side of the rope. But because he didn't try as often as some other teachers, it was easier thinking he was against me. The months following Mr. Wilks and Mr. Moyer's conversation, I had made up my mind that they all were against me, and it showed.

(At Terrell's home)

"This is the third phone call I've received this month concerning his behavior. Solomon, you told me things were changing with my son and I believed you."

"Ms. Hayes, consider the reports you received a few months ago. His homeroom teacher reported a change in Terrell that even you didn't believe. There's an explanation for this relapse."

"Maybe the explanation is standing here in front of me."

"I don't understand."

"I'm a direct woman, Solomon. With two sons, I have to be. You're an older man. Older than me and much older than my son. Perhaps that is why you don't connect with him as well as another mentor might."

"I understand Terrell. I understand his challenges, Ms. Hayes."

"Then you should understand American boys need things to keep them occupied. Music, sports, I'll even allow video games if it keeps him out the streets. You don't encourage any of this, Solomon. Not even sports. Now, I know you come highly recommended. But I also know that your work with the mentoring program is what's keeping you here in America. Understand Solomon, my son is my top priority." "You must understand, Ms. Hayes. It took Terrell many years and many experiences to become who he is today. It will take a similar length of time to change who he will become tomorrow. Music, sports, other forms of entertainment, I support all of these things. But first I must support Terrell and what he sees beneficial to himself. But you are correct, I will not give him a controller to a video game. For I believe the video game will ultimately control him more than he will control it. Terrell is on a path towards incredible things, Ms. Hayes. We must not put obstacles in his way because of fear."

"Are you calling me a fearful woman, Solomon?"

"I'm only acknowledging your reasons for fear. You have an African American teenager entering a stage in life where his very presence becomes the object of people's fear. And we've seen what people here do to things they're afraid of. Terrell is an asset to humanity. I want to show him, to convince him. I want to pull him from the game that has trapped him, not surround him with other games."

"What is this recent episode about, Solomon? Can you explain that to me? He was good for a while. Now he's back to his old self."

"I don't have the explanation, but there must be one."

There were more than one. I had a whole world of explanations, starting with being passed over for class leader.

(At school)

"Our new class leader, Brian Anderson, will coordinate the mid-semester festivals. Give him your undivided attention," said Mr. Wilks.

But there was nothing I needed to hear from Mr. Wilks or Brian. I didn't care about a mid-semester festival either. I stopped caring about school altogether. As far as I was concerned, the game was rigged and I was just taking up space. So when they all returned from lunch one day, they saw an empty desk where I used to sit.

That was the good thing about having lived on both sides of the rule book, when the good side rejected me, the bad side held their arms wide open.

"What are you doing out here, Terrell? This ain't you anymore," said one of the boys I used to smoke pot with, after seeing me creep out of one of the school's maintenance doors.

"That in there isn't me either," I responded while gesturing behind me towards the school. "So what are ya'll up to?"

"What are we always up to cuz . . ." "Yeah," I said. "I know."

I knew before even asking. I guess I knew before I even cut class to sneak outside. Nothing was ever new outside. The only opportunity for something new and different was in the classroom but that didn't seem to be working. But still, I knew my passport to the future wasn't across that field.

"Hey man, you coming or what?" he said before walking across the field towards their secret smoking area.

My heart was telling me no and my eyes were still staring at the doors I'd just walked out of.

The doors of the school opened both ways but at that point it didn't feel like it. Walking out was easy. I just nudged it open. It felt like I would need an entire football team to help me reopen it because of everything I thought was holding it closed. Unfairness, judgements, and hypercritical rules were all things I thought were holding the door shut, and I was convinced it wouldn't reopen. The more I believed it, the further away those doors seemed. So, I followed my friend across the field. We were walking to the other side of the football team's practice field. I could already smell the marijuana smoke. But that wasn't what caused me to fall.

"You alright man?" he asked. "I know you're not high just from smelling some of it."

"No, I'm good." I said. But I wasn't good at all. I looked down to see the little foot hole I tripped over and some things instantly came back to me.

In middle school we were all excited to play the conference championship on a high school field, especially me. All the excitement was probably why I didn't hear my coaches warn us about the foot holes and uneven field. I was going full speed when I fell, but as much as my ankle was hurting, thinking I would miss the rest of the most important game of middle school was even more painful. That's when I heard the voices for the very first time.

Sitting on that bench with my cleats off and ice on my ankle, I didn't realize there wasn't an actual man behind me talking to me.

"There is in this world no such force as the force of a person determined to rise," was what he said. I never looked behind me to see, with everyone in the stands yelling and cheering I thought it was some old man giving me a pep talk. Years later, ditching school and walking back across that same field, made me remember it all. It made me remember how my mom, my brother Malik, and even my football coach couldn't keep me on that bench. I needed to be in the game then. So how much more should I need to be in my high school classroom, I asked myself while picking myself up.

The marijuana was being passed around; it wasn't long before it got to me. Reaching out for it was easy, as easy as opening the door to ditch school. Why can being hard headed be so easy yet doing the right thing be so hard?

"Are you going to pass it or marry it?" one of guys asked. That question started a conversation among them that gave me even more to think about.

"I know you're not talking about passing something. Try passing the basketball sometimes."

"Try getting your own rebounds sometimes. You can sit out there and wait for a pass but you can't fight for rebounds?"

"Whatever."

They kept on and on about passing the basketball but rebounding stuck with me. Even against taller, stronger boys I was a good rebounder on the basketball court. They were always pushing and pulling on me, but I always rose for those rebounds even when I got hurt during the football game. I was able to rise and rebound from my injury fast enough to get back into the game. How come I can't rebound from Mr. Moyer's comments, I started asking myself. And what made his words too heavy to rise from? The answer probably would've come to me if I'd kept my mind clear. I ruined that chance. The marijuana I refused to let pass me by began to have its effects on me.

"You good?" somebody asked me.

Despite whatever my response was, I wasn't good. Not the kind of good I had proven I could be in school and not as good as I promised Malik I would be. He never wanted me to use drugs, not even smoke cigarettes. His eyes used to be as low as a sleeping cat and as red as ketchup bottle caps, but "don't do what I do," was all that ever came out of his mouth. Out of all the people I was disappointing by getting high, disappointing a brother behind bars should've been the last thing that made me sad; but it was the first thing.

I could still see the school's doors from where we were and I could barely hear the final bell ring. We watched everybody coming out of the doors like they were a crowd of brainwashed losers and the cloud of marijuana smoke above our heads represented the crown of winners. It didn't take much of a breeze for that crown to blow away. The cloud of anger over my mind took longer.

"So what's up, Terrell? Are you going to sprint down there to catch your bus or are you growing up today?"

I didn't know exactly what that meant but no matter what I wanted my answer to be, I wouldn't have made it to the buses on time.

The house we ended up at was barely even a house. It was more like one big room. There were no walls separating anything or anybody. Nobody was hiding. Nobody except me. The feeling from the marijuana was wearing off and I could see the horror show plain as day. The needles and noises were scary but the smell was horrible.

"Get back in here," one of them told me. "We got enough room over here."

I didn't know what they were finding room for, but I tried to find my phone. Solomon's phone number was still saved in my outgoing calls, and I needed to get away from that place. I knew what leaving meant. I knew what they would call me at school and how some of them might even treat me. It didn't matter. A whole lot was going to be lost in that place. My reputation among drug users was a loss I could live with. My consciousness was something different. I didn't know how it happened or even what really happened. But for a while, all my lights were out. When I came to, I was standing in an alley down the road from the drug house. I didn't know how I got there, but there was a voice in my head.

"There is in this world no such force as the force of a person determined to rise,"

I knew I hadn't risen to where I needed to be but from what I could remember, I rose up out of that dope house. That's a win in my book. Standing down that alley, I couldn't see the dope house anymore but I could still smell it on me. Then I saw headlights. I thought they were Phillip's, but they weren't. They were Mr. Solomon's. He could see it in my eyes and smelled it on my clothes as soon as I sat in his car. He didn't say anything. I didn't either. When he dropped me off at home he just handed me a little bottle of body spray.

"You smell like you might need this. Another Malik is the last thing your mother needs."

After saying "whatever" under my breath, I walked in the house. I woke up the next morning still not wanting to return to school. I definitely didn't want to be at the house Mr. Solomon picked me up from, but I knew I didn't want to be at school either. So I got ready for school like I normally would. I argued with Patrice over the bathroom, I watched my mom drive away and even though Patrice offered to drop me off at school on her way to college, it was easy convincing her I'd rather ride the bus. After she left, the house was all mine.

CHAPTER NINE

"Reality is wrong. Dreams are for real."
—Tupac Shakur

THERE WAS NOTHING better than pop-tarts and channel surfing with no sister or mom telling me "stop changing the channel and choose something." But during the weekdays there was nothing on TV except home improvement shows and the news. Before I could turn the channel from the news I saw a mugshot of a guy who looked just like my big brother. The news lady was saying to be on the lookout for him. After him, there were other faces, similar faces. I started channel surfing again until I found a music video marathon. I didn't need to surf any further after that. Rap has all the fast cars and fast lifestyles I wanted to see, the perfect combination of guys living the life and the girls that came with it.

It was amazing to see what girls would do for a guy with money. Going back to school seemed less and less important. None of them (rappers) were talking about getting an education. They weren't talking anything my mom, Mr. Solomon, or any of my teachers were talking about. It didn't seem to matter what kind of guy you were as long as you had money. There was one concert being aired where the rapper said,

"... you need to crawl before you ball, come and meet me in the bathroom stall, and show me why you deserve to have it all ..."

Those were his actual words and girls were responding to his

Andrew D Shepherd

lyrics as if he was passing out scholarships. My mom and aunts called this music disrespectful. But they never explained why disrespect worked so well. The chair I was watching the videos from was where mom would often sit and lecture me about being a gentleman, being respectful, and treating girls the right way.

"Purpose and Pleasure," she said. "Think of their purpose before your pleasure, Terrell. The world needs doctors, teachers, politicians, and wives, not more baby mamas."

With as many of my cousins who were single mothers, my mother had more than enough examples. But the videos I was watching didn't show what can come nine months later, not even a day later. Consequences didn't seem to matter, and neither did any of the school work I was losing my friends over. Making the honor society or Dean's List wasn't a part of anyone's song. No one was making it rain by throwing progress reports in the air. But before I made my mind up about school being a total waste of time, I saw something that made it look less like TV and more like real life.

Instead of seeing the crowd of screaming fans in the video, I focused on just one of them. She looked a lot like my sister, with less clothes and a lot more makeup, but still looked a lot like Patrice. I never noticed her before. I only saw the number of girls in the videos. I never singled out just one. That made her real, not just another object in the video like before, but a living breathing girl.

". . . you need to crawl before you ball, come and meet me in the bathroom stall, and show me why you deserve to have it all . . ."

As much as we argued, I didn't want to think of my sister following anyone into a bathroom stall just to prove she deserved anything. Her 4.0 GPA was proof of that. I didn't want to think it was even possible for her to believe anything else. But with the wrong influence, it was possible. Just as it was possible for me to overlook those kinds of lyrics that way.

In Juvie, when none of us boys paid the super serious mentors like

68

Mr. Solomon any attention, he once said, "Be careful of what music becomes your theme music. By the time you realize you need to turn your station, it may have already turned you."

I didn't want anything turning or manipulating me, and I didn't want anyone thinking I hated women either. My aunt called rap music that women-hating music. I didn't think it was women-hating music. I just thought some people didn't always see people as actual human beings. The next video was different but still the same. This time a different rapper said,

"Ass fat, yeah I know, you just got cash? Blow sum mo', blow sum mo', blow sum mo', the more you spend it, the faster it go, bad bitches, get on the floor . . ."

The woman rapping seemed to be right. The more money the guys threw in the air, the faster the   girls moved. It confused me. My mom said "consider their purpose not my pleasure" but in the music video, their purpose seemed to be the guys' pleasure. Even that summer, Mr. Solomon talked about the problem with boys treating girls like amusement parks, but I wasn't sure if he was right anymore. By saying "the faster it goes" instead of "the faster she goes," the woman rapping seemed to be identifying those other women as machines controlled by money.

I thought about my mom after that. I wondered if anyone looked at her or any part of her as an "it" instead of a person.

Even with the first video when the guy said, "meet me in the bathroom stall" I couldn't think anyone could watch my mom go to work, come home, cook a family dinner and then go to night school. And after all of that, still think about taking her into some bathroom stall. They should name that building after her instead. But most of us didn't think about girls in that way, the right way. At least not right away. That kind of forward thinking wasn't part of our daily reality. That's when I heard;

"Reality is wrong. Dreams are for real," It was a voice I easily

recognized. My aunt had the biggest crush on Tupac Shakur so I watched more of his videos as a kid than any others. But still, reality being wrong and dreams being right didn't make any sense. It sounded like wishful thinking until I considered the things I wished for. They were good things: a future, my mom to be happy, and to be able to take care of myself—things that should be reality. And that's when it hit me. Tupac was talking about the things that should be as if they were reality, because they can be. All our dreams could be real, and should be.

My sister had many dreams that were coming true, but one didn't. It should have. The night of her senior prom was one she dreamed about. But going to the prom with a girl who wasn't putting out didn't sound too dreamy to her boyfriend, Shawn. Weeks leading up to the big dance, all I heard was my sister and her girlfriends talk about was the prom and how their night would go. I knew they were dreaming. In reality, most upperclassmen boys weren't interested in the innocent stuff they wanted to do. Even I knew that. And I was right.

"You must be dreaming," was the last thing I heard Shawn tell Patrice after hearing her plan to share a hotel room with her girlfriends instead of with him. What was she thinking, I thought? I thought wrong. Patrice was the only one who was thinking, thinking about her future. See, Shawn was right when he said my sister must have been dreaming. She had a four- year dream that was coming true. It never included his hotel room.

My mom was upset about not having the prom pictures they were all looking forward to seeing, and my aunts wanted someone to blame for Patrice being stood up that night. But Shawn wasn't there to be blamed. He was out somewhere making his life imitate the art we all had grown used to. That art didn't include waiting for sex or being a part of a happiness that wasn't our own. Reality was wrong. But the dreams could be real for those like my sister, who don't compromise them for the present, temporary reality.

CHAPTER TEN

"Why is it that, as a culture, we are more comfortable seeing two men holding guns than holding hands?"

—*Ernest Gaines*

A WEEK HAD PASSED since I skipped class to smoke across the football field and needed Mr. Solomon to pick me up from that horrible smelling drug house. That was a lesson well learned, and the lesson I learned from watching those music videos and hearing those words from Tupac Shakur—being back in school felt right. But I didn't expect to get away scott-free.

"So you took a vacation day last week, Mr. Hayes?"

"No Sir, Mr. Hail. My stomach was killing me. I could barely get out of bed."

I'd lied to teachers many times in the past but I wanted that to be a part of my old *reality*.

"So your mother knew?" he asked.

That was my opportunity to come clean. But I was still in the crawl phase of accepting responsibility.

"I didn't want her missing work, sir. You know how it can be."
"Well she could've brought you home some medicine, Pepto-Bismol maybe."

"Umm, she had a bottle left in the pantry; it helped. Actually sir, that's how I made it today."

Instead of standing there smiling as if I've pulled off some grand heist, I should've walked away.

"So Terrell . . . you're ok now?"

"One hundred percent, Mr. Hail."

"That's good, Terrell. I'm happy that blue syrup could help, I can't stand Pepto-Bismol."

"Whatever it takes to get back into class."

When he stood there and paused, I should've known I'd messed up and confessed. Instead, I kept that stupid smile on my face.

"One hundred percent, huh Mr. Hayes. How about the battery life of your cell phone? Is that also at one hundred percent? If so, Google Pepto-Bismol for me."

I googled it and saw that Pepto-Bismol is a pink liquid, not blue. For some reason, Mr. Hail gave me a break. Accepting responsibility would have been a lot easier than the shame I felt lying to someone trying to help me. But I forgot about all that as soon as I got into class. I was still mad about being passed over for class leader. So when Brian, the new class leader, asked for ideas on how to improve the school, I kept mine to myself. If they wanted my ideas, they would've made me class leader; and I wasn't the only one thinking that.

Guys in the back were whispering the same thing, and Brian didn't even look like a leader. His mother still made him bag lunches, nobody was going to follow that. I tried holding onto the guidance I got from the voices, especially the man who said *"If you're paid before you walk on the court, what's the point in playing as if your life depended on it?"* But that sounded like just another bag lunch, something to keep me full and quiet while I'm being treated unfairly.

"Our Hold On program is something that no one participates in but Mr. Wilks has found a way to help me change that." Brian said.

Hold On was a program that asked students to acknowledge other students who were falling behind in some way. We were supposed to pull that person into a circle of support and convince them to "Hold

On." The program didn't get much play in our school. The ones who needed help weren't comfortable sharing, and the ones who could help weren't confident anyone would listen. And nobody, I mean nobody, was ok with standing in a circle in high school. No one except Brian. What Brian and Mr. Wilks had in mind, being confident or comfortable, didn't matter.

"Mr. Wilks gave me a list of students for the Hold On program. Between bells, I'll talk to as many as I can. For extra credit, you can all help. The purpose is to show other students that help is everywhere, so we will be everywhere."

No matter how Brian explained it, it felt like the purpose was to show others students how nosey and weird we could be. Especially the holding hands part of it.

"Holding hands is an important part. Hold On means we're holding on to each other, hand to hand."

"We can't just lock arms?" I asked.

"Standing around in a circle is weird enough." one of the other students said.

Right after he said that, the thing I thought would happen did happen.

"What in the world is this!" someone yelled from down the hall. After a few seconds he wasn't alone. It seemed like half the school had something to say about our group encouragement techniques. Brian didn't care. Being called names and getting laughed at wasn't his concern, but it was mine.

"Talking to each other about doing better is one thing," I said "but holding hands in the hallways . . . in front of everybody?"

But that's when I saw it for the first time. He was like Mr. Solomon and his clothes and car. Brian didn't care what people thought. Not in a rebelliously self-conscious way that most of us "didn't care," Brian really just didn't care. Reputation, sports, friends, even girlfriend; none of those he wanted, so none of us owned him. He was lucky like that. He wasn't wearing our shackles. His skater shoes looked like flat tires and his clothes looked homemade. I bet the bicycle he rode to school cost more than everything in his closet, but not mine. My closet was filled with shackles and Polo shirts.

I was thinking a lot about that on the bus ride home, about being jealous of Brian for not caring about the things I cared about. Even though I gave my new clothes back to my mom, that was more me feeling bad than actually growing up. By the time the bus got to my house I realized I was mostly jealous of Brian because he wasn't jealous of anyone else. No music video or reality TV showed the reality Brian wanted. That was the moment I understood what Mr. Solomon meant when he told me "when you can say 'I'm satisfied,' no one can sell you anything."

Teenagers like me were sold on how we needed to look since I wanted my first pair of Jordan's. But boys like Brian weren't buying it, even though he was probably the only one who could afford to buy them.

"Why are you always around, man?!" was the first thing I heard yelled that next morning at school. When I followed the small crowd around the corner, all I saw was a group of guys surrounding Brian. The first thing I thought was how hard it would be for Brian to "hold on" to a group of boys that wanted to beat him up, but at my own risk I yelled.

"Chill out, y'all!. He's just doing what Mr. Wilks told him to do."

"Mr. Wilks told him to come up behind people grabbing their hands and stuff?" one of them asked me.

I wanted to tell them to just get over it but, by the way, their fists were balled up, that didn't seem like a good idea and after all, Brain and I weren't exactly friends. But I stood there with him, waiting and hoping for a teacher to tell us to clear the hallways, but no one came. The longer we stood there the more those boys looked ready to fight. But soon I heard from one of my teachers, but not the ones I could see.

"Why is it that, as a culture, we are more comfortable seeing two men holding guns than holding hands?"

I wasn't sure of how that was supposed to help Brain or myself until I started noticing some of their hands. Their fists were balled up but not balled very tight. They wanted to let it go. They wanted to let the reason for fighting go, they just needed help. It reminded me of what Mr. Solomon said about scared people holding guns.

"That's why their hands shake, Terrell. Because they are only thinking violence is a 'man' thing to do. But most of them would rather have someone to squeeze instead of a trigger."

Mr. Solomon was right. Making fists seemed like the "man" thing to do, but it wasn't and they knew it. I guess they had to walk away as if they were letting Brian and me off the hook, but I knew better. I just didn't let my fearless class leader know that.

"What you doing, Brian? Walking up and holding people's hands, you know how weird that is?"

He just looked at me and walked away. I walked the opposite direction, towards Mr. Wilks' class.

"I wanted to be a team player, Mr. Wilks. I really did. But unless we get us some bodyguards, I can't do this with Brian. He's not from around here" was the speech I rehearsed on the way to class that next morning. But Brian beat me to it.

"Well, class, today is a day of firsts," was how Mr. Wilks began class that day.

Brian sat on the front right side of the classroom where I couldn't see his face. I kept trying to see his expression when Mr. Wilks said he was no longer able to be class leader. I was focused on Brian for so long I didn't hear Mr. Wilks ask the class for volunteers to be class leader. By then it wouldn't have mattered. I'd let my grades slip below the highest average. It was another one of those slides, Mr. Solomon mentioned. The ones you can't just slide back up. And over the next few weeks, I wasn't the only one sliding.

"Brian, quitting has always been habit forming, but I didn't know that you would be another example." Mr. Wilks said after an exam that Brian bombed.

Brian didn't show any emotion after that. But it wasn't the "whatever" shoulder shrug I used to give; it was something else.

"What's up with you, man? Won't your folks spaz out over your grades dropping like this?" I asked.

It was weird seeing the "hold on" kid needing someone to hold on to him. It was weird for him, too.

"What do you care, Terrell? You and your friends make fun of every good thing."

"A bunch of us holding hands in the hallway, hardly a good look, Brian."

"Hold On wasn't about a good look; it was about a good thing. In Hyderabad, India, where I'm from, nothing is a 'good look.' But men are taught to hold hands to show togetherness and support. It works because how it looks doesn't matter when no one is looking. You all look at everything and you hope it gives you a reason to laugh. Laughing the medication out of medicine is all you're doing"

I stood there looking at Brian as if I didn't know what he was talking about. I kept the look going for as long as it took for his frustration to carry him off; it took longer than I thought it would. He kept standing there because he expected me to understand. I did understand, and he was right. Laughing the medication out of medicine was all we did. In ISS, anytime a teacher began getting through to a student, something was done or said to get everyone laughing and to get the student's mind off improving. Every time one of my friends thought about obeying the rules, somebody was there to laugh that idea away, too. Our comic relief relieved us of a lot of chances to help each other.

CHAPTER ELEVEN

"There is no obstacle in the path of young people who are poor or members of minority groups that hard work and preparation cannot cure."

—*Barbara Jordan*

BY THE END of my junior year I'd gotten use to the voices but hadn't learned to fully depend on them. This lady mentioned hard work and preparation as a "cure," like it was medicine. That had to mean being lazy and refusing to prepare for what I wanted was a sickness. I didn't want to believe I was sick. I still wanted to believe it was someone else's fault. The more I thought about what the lady said and what Brian said, the harder it got to blame everyone else. But it didn't mean I didn't try.

Almost a whole semester had passed since Mr. Moyer convinced Mr. Wilks to pass me over for class leader but I kept what Mr. Moyer said about me fresh in my head. Even when the lady's message about overcoming obstacles tried to replace it, my resentment kept pushing me to mess up. The tighter I held it, the more my grades slipped, and that didn't bother me. As far I was concerned, I had spent the first part of the year proving I could be as smart as any other student. I was ready to spend the rest of my junior year like I spent the beginning of my sophomore year.

But spending all that time staying out of trouble caused my adult-radar to shut off. Skipping class wasn't as easy anymore.

"Terrell Hayes!" I heard while turning a corner. "Are you going for a stroll?"

One thing about skipping class was the halls were usually empty.

That meant no one was usually around to signal Mr. Hail. "Something like that, sir." I answered.

"Something like that? Is that the best you can come up with? You're not out looking for more Pepto-Bismol are you?"

I'd already lied to Mr. Hail once; I wasn't going to do it again. "Well, if you're just going to stand around, let's find a better place for you to stand," he said.

I never expected to get away with skipping class, I don't think I was even trying to get away with it. I was happy to get back to where I was the for sure class leader—ISS. Walking back into ISS felt good after being gone for almost a year. But the welcome back didn't feel as good once I saw who the teacher was.

"What's all the whispering for? Are we celebrating Terrell's return? Well let's just stand up and clap for him. Backwards progress should always be congratulated, I guess."

Mr. Moyer always had something to say. He acted like it was tough love, but I knew hate when I heard it.

"It's not mine or any other teacher's expectation that matters, it's what you expect of yourself."

Mr. Moyer was one those teachers who talked to you without looking at you. It was no point in trying to explain anything to him and he wasn't the only one throwing shade my way. Deon, one of the ISS regulars, had an opinion, too.

"What are you doing back in here? Heard you were headed for the honor roll list?"

In ISS they knew everyone's business, especially the people who were changing up.

"It's no big deal, Deon. Just some stupid homework," I said.

"Na, it wasn't just some homework. You were going for the class leader spot."

"Who told you that?"
"It don't matter who. You didn't get it, did you?"
"Brian got it."
"His grades were better?"
"Not at the time."

"Brian wasn't in Juvi his freshman year, that's what it was. You get it now? That honor roll class leader crap, that isn't you. This is you right here."

The bell rang before I could agree with him. I didn't want to agree with him. I didn't want to agree with Mr. Moyer either. But I couldn't deny wanting to be class leader. I wanted to stand out, in a good way for a change. I thought I earned that much.

"You've got to get to the stage in life where going for it is more important than winning or losing."—Arthur Ashe

It took me a while to understand that one. Getting to the stage where just going for it is the most important thing didn't make any sense. Sounded a lot like setting myself up for disappointment. Later I would understand more. Mr. Hail had a way of making people understand things.

"Mr. Hayes, I'm glad that I caught up with you out here. It is here (ISS) that I wanted to talk to you about. Why were you back in ISS? You were roaming the halls yesterday when I found you. What were you looking for?"

"I wasn't looking for anything, Mr. Hail."

"No, I didn't think you were. I think you were hiding."

"Hiding? I ain't afraid of nobody!"

"You mean, you aren't afraid of anybody and that's not what I'm talking about. We're so preoccupied with not being punks we don't see when we're being punked."

"Huh?"

"I'm talking about progression, son. I spoke with your homeroom teacher, Mr. Wilks. He said you've turned the corner. He said your progression last semester was more than any other student's. And then you did something even more stunning."

"What?"

"You started skipping class again. After religiously completing your assignments, you began backsliding. So, I'm asking; does progression scare you? Does the fear of being different from your friends scare you?"

"I am different," I responded as convincingly as I could. But even I wasn't convinced anymore.

"You only flirt with being different. The fact that you were in here today shows that you're not committed to change."

This wasn't the first time Mr. Hail cornered me somewhere and gave me my whole life story. Just as I did with my mom and aunts, I tried to tune him out; but Mr. Hail was a juvenile detention counselor before becoming vice principal. He didn't quit as easy as the rest of them, especially when he knew we wanted him to.

"You remind me a lot of Josh McClellan, Terrell. Do you remember him?"

"No."

"You're not the only one who's forgotten who Josh was. Six years ago, Josh forgot who he was, too. Josh forgot that he was a leader, and so he began following others. Not following the crowd so much but following what the crowd expected of him. Do you know who was in the crowd?"

"No, sir."

"Your brother, Malik. He and Josh were as tight as two young men could be. When Josh would miss basketball practice to feel his lungs with marijuana smoke, Malik was right there. Smoking with him. Joking with him. Being each other's biggest fan. But once Josh found out some college scouts were interested in him, smoking and skipping practice no longer seemed like the thing to do. But your brother, he wasn't feeling the change. Malik missed his smoking buddy. Even after Josh started breaking school records, Malik only missed his smoking buddy. So what do you think happened when Josh started having problems on the basketball court or in the classroom? Do you think Malik reminded Josh about college and the opportunities he had in front of him? Do you think Malik told his friend to work harder, bite down, and stay focused? Or did he tell Josh how much he still misses his smoking buddy? By the end of that basketball season, instead of Norfolk State getting the star two-guard they were hoping for, Malik got his smoking buddy back. The basketball team started losing and Josh gave up. He just stopped going for it. Do you think those college scouts were interested in our team's record or Josh's effort, Terrell?"

That bus ride home took longer than usual. What the voice said about "going for it is more important than winning and losing," was making a lot of sense. Going for the class leader position forced me to have one of the highest averages in my junior class, I should've paid more attention to that. When I got home, I walked past my brother's room and saw some things on his wall that I hadn't paid attention to in a long time. Before I walked in;

"There is no obstacle in the path of young people who are poor or members of minority groups that hard work and preparation cannot cure" was said to me again. That time I heard it while looking at some drawings that Malik and I started when I was just starting elementary school. It was comic books, but with heroes from our favorite sports teams. NBA players were Malik's favorite, especially Lebron James. I remembered how mad he was when the Cavs lost to the Boston Celtics. But even that didn't compare to when his idol decided to go down and play for the Heat. I don't know how many times mom had to calm him down. But when the art program at his junior high school went away because of funding, so did our comic book.

The school wasn't giving away anymore art supplies and my mom didn't have the extra money. It affected Malik a lot. He felt the school had taken something from him. He never came out and said it. Instead, he kept telling everyone how he didn't "have time for stupid comic books anyway". I suppose that was easier than admitting to how he really felt. Blaming the school and giving up was easier too, but I was beginning to see that those were Malik's choices. They weren't choices made for him.

Our school may have been one of the low income schools losing a lot of its programs, but we still knew how to draw. A school with no programs didn't mean students with no potential, and that night was when I heard,

It is better to be prepared for an opportunity and not have one than to have an opportunity and not be prepared."—Whitney Young

With that in mind I started preparing.

That night, as a high school junior with no art program, I decided to finish those comic books. Malik began them with his favorite athletes and added a hip-hop twist to it. I removed the twist and replaced it with a straight line to our heritage. The voices I'd been hearing were not from this generation, but they were still about to guide me to better decisions. So, I used the popularity of basketball players to voice the messages I'd been receiving, and it was awesome.

But instead of the NBA gymnasiums, I held the games at our neighborhood park. I had Steph Curry lighting up threes while telling kids that character is more important than fancy cars. I had Lebron James dunking on kids after explaining how people who look for excuses will always find one. It was going to be awesome but I needed more coloring and sketching material. The next day at school one of the teachers in ISS hooked me up. They always kept things laying around to keep us busy. And I was busy. I don't remember eating lunch that day, just using an entire table in the cafeteria for my project and it was nearly finished until,

"Everyone exit the building, immediately!" came over the intercom. If I didn't see everyone moving, I would've thought it was in my head. But this was real. And what some freshman did was real stupid. Smoking in the faculty bathroom was dumb enough, but dropping the cigarette in the trash instead of the toilet was what we called freshman-foolish. It wasn't until I was rushed across the parking lot that I remembered I left all the comic book material on the table. I hope they don't burn up, I remember thinking. But those sheets of paper were nowhere near the small trashcan fire. By the time they let us inside the school, they were nowhere to be found either.

That was all I needed. The last thing I wanted was for a wannabe comedian using my stuff for his senior class standup comic material, like I would've once done. But I wasn't tripping over that, I did what I set out to do. I picked up where my brother left off, and made it better. Whoever grabbed it will at least have learned something. I learned a lack of resources at our school didn't mean a lack of talent. A lack of resources only stops those who can be stopped.

CHAPTER TWELVE

"Stumbling is not falling,"

—Malcolm X

I FELT PRETTY GOOD after I attempted the comic book, even though I didn't finish it. But the win started making me look at my brother like a loser for quitting the way he did. That was when I heard another familiar voice, and a serious one.

"Stumbling is not falling," he said.

By that time, I was starting to understand the voices better. So I believed if all Malik did was stumble, he could've regained his balance. And artwork was something he enjoyed back when he was "balanced". So, there I was thinking of how to redo the comics that I lost at school and thinking of a way to get them to Malik. Asking my mom to mail them wasn't an option. Mr. Solomon was the only option I could think of. When I heard the front door opening, I thought it was him but Mr. Solomon only had one key on his keychain. My mom had the janitor's set.

The frantic rattling of keys at the front door meant she was in a rush to get inside. Which usually meant she was in a rush to get at me. I hadn't been on my A-game at school and her coming home late could've only meant she'd already found out. When it came to satisfying my mom, looking busy or being busy were the only two answers. But the two things I was busy doing, thinking about Malik and thinking about how to send him some positive comics, weren't busy enough. Just thinking about doing something wasn't enough. It wasn't "the thought that counts" in my mom's house, especially with what I was thinking about.

"Letters, Terrell? Your grades are starting to look like your sophomore year and instead of focusing on your assignments you're asking me about sending a letter to a prison."

"They're comics, Ma. And not to the prison but to Malik. It's actually a good thing I'm doing if you would check it out. Mr. Solomon has been helping me understand some quotes from African American leaders in the past. They're pretty good, Ma. So, I decided to make them the dialogue for the comic book but with famous ball players reciting them instead of civil rights leaders. Like Lebron, Steph, Melo—all those guys. Plus, a lot has changed in the league since Malik left. I would be keeping him up to date."

"Did Lebron leave Cleveland to go to prison? If not, then what in the world can he do for your brother?"

She wouldn't even say Malik's name anymore; it was always "your brother" or "that boy."

"And I'm sick of you talking about that boy like he left for college or the military! Your brother is in prison, Terrell. Prison! So you tell me how your *art* is going to change any of that?"

"You used to like art, Ma. Listening to you brag on Malik is what made me want to do it. Just because you don't talk about him anymore doesn't mean I can't keep drawing."

"What's there to talk about, Terrell? My son, the drug dealer?"

"We don't even go and see him like we used to."

"Don't you start with that. You know good and well why that is. I was bringing him meals and pictures. Normal family things, Terrell. What did he convince you to sneak him? Dirty magazines and a stupid little cell phone that he knew he couldn't have in there. You could've been in a cell right next to him. Did either of you think about that, you being in there with those animals?"

"Malik isn't an animal, Mom."

"But he's in a cage, isn't he?"

Mirrors

She left me in Malik's room looking at his artwork and mine. They were similar, very similar. I think Mom was afraid that Malik and I were just as similar. But she was right about how casual I saw prison. It wasn't a big deal to me, to any of us (my friends). I knew more people who had family members locked up than I knew who didn't. We (my friends) saw it like Juvi or ISS—just another part of life. But a voice changed that. It wasn't loud like the others, but when I saw her in the reflection of Malik's window, it was loud and clear.

"Jails and prisons are designed to break human beings, to convert the population into specimens in a zoo - obedient to our keepers, but dangerous to each other."

Besides her afro, she looked like my mom. And like my mom, when she talked I had to listen.

"Jails and prisons are designed to break human beings, to convert the population into specimens in a zoo . . ."

I went to the zoo once and the first thing I thought about was how the animals looked so calm in the cages. Why weren't they growling and clawing to get out? Then I thought about a guy who was in a booth next to Malik the first time we visited him in prison. The guy wouldn't stop crying and beating on the window. By the time the guards grabbed him, his knuckles were already bleeding.

I didn't see him the next visit. Or the ones after that. But during our last visit with Malik, I saw him again. He was so different. So much calmer, like he knew where he was and who the prison expected him to be. It was a lot like those zoo animals. Whatever he was before prison or whatever he was supposed to be in life, the zookeepers broke him from that. I wanted my brother to come home, but not broken by his zookeepers.

A lot of what the lady with the afro said stuck with me, especially the part about *"obedient to our keepers, but dangerous to each other."*

My boy, Justin, was like that, too. In Juvie, he learned to listen and be obedient to the attendants (guards). We all did. But what Justin wouldn't do to guards, he did to everyone else.

I was his boy, and after a couple of months, everyone else was auditioning for my job. But back then, I didn't feel like an animal. I bet Justin didn't either. We were just surviving. I suppose behaving is surviving when someone else has the keys to your cage, but that's what we did then and there. Here and now, free and at home, was supposed to be the time to do better. But I was still staring at Malik's drawings and comparing them to my own wondering if I was on the same path. Then I heard;

" *Start where you are. Use what you have. Do what you can.*"

He made perfect sense. I didn't see his reflection like I did the woman's, but I knew it was the guy with the glasses and tennis racket. He'd spoken to me the most, so I knew his voice. Comparing Malik's drawings to mine and comparing where he was with where I'd been was pointless. Malik made mistakes carving out his own path. He didn't know there was one already carved. He'd never heard of all the people that I've been hearing from.

"Start where you are," he said.

It meant change starts today. He didn't want me to worry about yesterday.

"Use what you have."

He was telling me if I didn't have it then I didn't have to have it. My family, Mr. Solomon, school, and everything I needed to make better choices was surrounding me. I was apprehended by encouragers. So, the money, better school, and better opportunities I thought I needed were just excuses with handle bars, hoping I'd reach for one or all.

And "do what you can."

I didn't have to do it all. I didn't have to change the way my brother thought about himself or even the way some of the teachers thought about me. I just needed to change the way I thought about myself. The next morning while I was walking down the halls, I made my mind up to *start* back where I was, but the bad decisions I made after hearing Mr. Moyer talking to Mr. Wilks over a semester ago still had more consequences.

"Terrell Hayes, report to the Vice Principal's office," came across the intercom. I knew it wasn't just in my head by the way everyone was looking at me. Mr. Hail was known for letting us sit outside his office for hours before giving us an ISS slip or just chewing us out. But I had already served my time in ISS so I didn't know what I was there for.

Then I saw Tawanna leaving Mr. Hails office. Tawanna's last name is Daniels and as rumors of Tawanna, Cory, and Justin circulated, some of the football players started calling her TD. This wasn't because of her initials. Scoring "Touchdowns" on and off the field were a big thing and Tawanna's name began to appear on everyone's score card. They were lying. I knew Tawanna. Despite what happened the summer after our sophomore year, I still believed I knew Tawanna. We just hadn't talked in a long time.

"Tawanna, you're not walking out with slip?" I asked.

"This isn't for ISS, Terrell. He's on some other stuff."

Before I could ask what that other stuff was, his thunderous voice summoned me into his office. It made my stomach knot up. I thought about Pepto-Bismol but I wasn't crazy enough to bring that up. When I walked in Mr. Hail's office it wasn't filled with college football and Golden Glove boxing trophies like before. He had artwork everywhere, some pretty cool stuff.

"Mr. Hayes, what do you see here?"

"Umm, drawings?"

"Drawings? That's all you see?"

"No sir, I see very good drawings."

Flattery worked sometimes with my mom. Mr. Hail was obviously not my mom.

"These are depictions, Mr. Hayes. Students from a small Literary Arts program upstate depicted these images based on how they see their school and their environment. I'm starting a similar program here. That is why you're in my office today."

Hearing Mr. Hail talk about me doing something that I enjoy went against every hunch I had before walking into his office.

"Mr. Moyer came to see me. He's convinced that you have communication issues. He's convinced that's the source of your continued academic backsliding."

"I communicate fine, Mr. Hail. Mr. Moyer just don't like anyone talking at all."

"Perhaps it's time to talk on paper. Tawanna Daniels will be my artist and you will be my scribe."

"Scribe?"

"Scribes were used once to maintain a record of civilization. Here, you will do something similar. But instead of writing how things are, you will write how thing ought to be."

"Mr. Hail, I can't just make up a new world?"

"Sure you can," he said as he stood up and walked towards his file cabinet. And there it was. My drawings that disappeared from the cafeteria. But it wasn't the pictures he was interested in.

"How you described scenarios of athletes giving such influential advice, I like that, Mr. Hayes. I like it a lot. I even felt like I've read some of what they were saying before. Like Dwayne Wade saying that "education is a passport to the future" after a slam dunk."

"I like that one too, sir."

"Look behind you, Mr. Hayes."

I did and there it was, a picture of a Malcolm X with those words underneath him.

Mr. Hayes, now I need you to repeat what you did with your drawings; but now you will add your meaning of these influential words. I want the positive voices of yesterday and today to speak to everyone who comes through the doors of this school. There will be a billboard out front every week. You will make sure it's not blank."

Having my words on a billboard every week wasn't what I had in mind, but Mr. Hail's word was law and always final.

"What should I call it?" I asked.

"Penned Influences. With pens, pencils, paint brushes, and even video equipment, we will give a better picture of society. Life at New Jefferson High School imitates all types of art. It's time we began influencing that art."

CHAPTER THIRTEEN

"The impulse to dream was slowly beaten out of me by experience. Now it surged up again and I hungered for books, new ways of looking and seeing."

—*Richard Wright*

WALKING INTO HOMEROOM late without being in trouble felt good for a change, but the way Tawanna was looking at me wasn't the kind of change I was expecting.

"This is your fault," she whispered. "I don't want to be a part of some stupid art project."

"And I did? Drawing is my thing, but Mr. Hail made me a scribe. I feel like I should be wearing a robe and sandals."

"You're going to be wearing a hospital robe if you don't get me out of this."

"This isn't my fault. I don't know why he chose us."

As I continued going back and forth with Tawanna about why we were chosen for that project, someone reminded me that I was chosen long before entering Mr. Hail's office.

"It is better to be prepared for an opportunity and not have one than to have an opportunity and not be prepared."

But that didn't sound like the opportunity I was looking for. The only person more skeptical than me was my mother, for obvious reasons.

(At home after school)
"And you're telling me they want you to be in charge of this?" "Yes, mom."

"And it's not any kind of disciplinary thing?"
"No, mom. I'm just reporting what I see in the school and stuff." She eventually let it go. But that was more than I could say for Tawanna. That entire week of school she looked at me like I was the grinch that stole her junior year. But eventually, she realized what I already knew. Mr. Hail's word was law.

"So," she said to me first thing one Monday morning, "what do you want to do, Terrell? Just start drawing stuff or what?"
"I guess, and I'll be writing stuff." "This is so wack."

"Whatever keeps Mr. Hail off our backs. Right?" "Whatever."

I didn't think Tawanna was going to roll with this much longer. I knew her. She would rather sit in ISS for a week than do something that didn't make sense to her. But then, in the midst of our complaining, we looked down the hall at something that made even less sense.

"You think you're the teacher's assistant, huh?" a student said pushing another one.

"Every time it's time to earn extra credit your hand goes up with an answer."

"So if I see your hand raised again, I'll raise mine. Right upside your head."

I didn't know those girls but Tawanna did. "You're not going down there are you?" I said.

"I ain't just gonna stay here while they mess with my girl, Terrell."
"We got permission to be out of class to do what Mr. Hail wanted us to do, I don't see fighting on this list anywhere."

Words of wisdom don't mean much when you see your friend shoved against a vending machine. Yells of "stop it" and "quit it" combined with nearly every curse word Tawanna could think of reached the vending machine area before we did. Luckily, so did a couple of teachers. After the fight was broken up and Tawanna calmed down, one of the teachers was actually willing to hear my explanation for us being in the hallway. Given our history of bad behavior and the language they just heard from the project leader (Tawanna), more convincing was needed.

Maybe if we hadn't gone into Mr. Hail's office right after the students who were fighting, Mr. Hail would've been in a better mood. But I doubted it.

"So this is how you two handle responsibility? I give you task, something different from your peers and this is how you use the opportunity? To play the vigilante hall monitors instead of the invisible reporters I assigned you to be."

"I spent a year of being invisible."

The office got dead silent after Tawanna spoke without being asked to. A few of Mr. Hail's plants even withered away in fear, I thought. After seeing him wipe the fog from his glasses and put them back on, I figured one of us would wither away in a minute.

"This program has been proven to be in the right hands. If your hands aren't suitable for the task, tell me now. There are always others to choose from . . ."

The lecture went on and every time I'd glance over at Tawanna, she looked less and less committed to the project. But before he ended, Mr. Hail's demanding voice was interrupted by another one;

"The impulse to dream was slowly beaten out of me by experience. Now it surged up again and I hungered for books, new ways of looking and seeing."

I was still looking at Tawanna when those words fell onto my ears. It was easy to see who they were meant for. Her body language screamed "I don't want to do this," and Mr. Hail was ready to give her what she wanted—but I couldn't let him.

"We got it, Mr. Hail," I rushed to say. "We understand what is expected of us."

Leaving his office with no ISS slip and the project still intact was more than I expected but for Tawanna, well;

"Since when do I need you or anyone else to speak for me?"

I wanted to tell her that people have been speaking for me all month. I wanted to tell her how appearances and voices of strangers became the voice of reason that I never had before. But Tawanna didn't believe in miracles, and why would she? When most of everyone else in school was playing tough (like me) or trying to build a reputation (like me), Tawanna spent most of her life trying not to.

"The ghetto is a trampoline for people using it for street credibility, it's quicksand for us who use it as an address," was the tattoo on Tawanna's arm. Most students thought it was one of her rap lyrics because Tawanna was known for freestyling and poetry since elementary school. She stopped doing both after it all happened. She would say she had grown out of it, but I knew the truth. Tawanna's older brother, Kevin used to hang with my other brother, Malik. Kevin wasn't from our part of town. Malik and some of Malik's friends knew that and they loved it. They thought bringing Kevin to parties and cookouts gave them some level of street credibility.

Kevin's parents thought friends like my brother and teenagers from my side of town would provide a better environment. That's when I learned that the mind's environment is more important than where you're actually at. My brother and his boys wanted to claim where Kevin came from and Kevin wanted the easier environment of my brother and his friends. The night everyone tried to get what they wanted, Kevin was the only unfamiliar face at some fancy house party that got out of control. Once everyone was identified, it was easy for the landlord to convince the police that he only shot Kevin in self-defense. There was no convincing Kevin's parents or his sister, Tawanna.

That and other things gave us a lot in common but for Penned Influences to do any good, we needed more to come together over than the brothers we'd lost. That's when I heard those words again;

Mirrors

"The impulse to dream was slowly beaten out of me by experience. Now it surged up again and I hungered for books, new ways of looking and seeing."

What happened to Kevin stopped Tawanna from dreaming or believing in anything? I didn't see a way to get her to believe in the Penned Influences project, even though I knew she would be better at influencing others than me. Then I remembered something else she did better than me, something she hadn't done since her brother died—rap. Our middle school freestyle champ hung it all up when her brother was taken but I knew she still had it in her.

Unfortunately, all the rap battles done in our hallways were about sex and money and Tawanna wasn't about that. That's how my Aunt's Tupac crush paid off. All those hours riding in the back seat, I remembered some positive lyrics of his and it was worth the risk pulling out my phone to find them.

"I got love for my brother, but we can never go nowhere unless we share with each other. We gotta start makin' changes. Learn to see me as a brother 'stead of 2 distant strangers. And that's how it's supposed to be. How can the Devil take a brother if he's close to me? I'd love to go back to when we played as kids but things changed, and that's the way it is."—Tupac Shakur

With Tupac dying before we were even born, I didn't expect Tawanna to know the song. I just hoped using hip hop from a conscious rapper like Tupac would remind Tawanna of how influential words can be if used correctly. I was wrong on both ends. She turned and said;

"'I see no changes. All I see is racist faces. Misplaced hate makes disgrace to races, we under, I wonder what it takes to make this one better place . . . let's erase the wasted."—Tupac Shakur

After surprising me by finishing that twenty-year-old rap verse, she said.

"And that's what they're doing, Terrell, erasing the wasted. Erasing fools like my brother who wasted his life. Locking up fools like your brother, for wasting his. Kevin used to like him some old school Tupac. But ain't no dead man's song gonna change where he's at now. Neither will us pretending to care about Mr. Hail's 'save the world' project."

While riding the bus home that day, I thought about what Tawanna said and it made sense. A song from Tupac or anyone else wouldn't bring her brother back or get mine out of jail. So what's the point of it, I thought. Mr. Hail wanted Penned Influences to write a new script for our lives. That sounded good but if we couldn't turn the page on today, how could we even get to tomorrow, I thought. Then a familiar voice reminded me of something.

"Start where you are. Use what you have. Do what you can."

I heard it but I pretended to not hear it, something I did with everyone. But he repeated himself.

"Start where you are. Use what you have. Do what you can."

He was right the first time. He wasn't telling me this because I thought I was on the same path as Malik, like before. These words came specifically because I needed to learn how to apply them to my everyday life.

When Mr. Hail put us in charge of Penned Influences, I was thinking about changing too much at one time. Getting Tawanna more committed to the project needed to be my second priority. I needed to be the first. I had let my grades slip and even though Mr. Hail didn't hold that against me when giving Tawanna and I this project, my mom and Mr. Solomon had expectations of me. Whether I always wanted to admit it or not, I've developed expectations of myself.

Mirrors

When the bus arrived at my house someone distracted me from getting out of my seat.

"We know the road to freedom has always been stalked by death."

It was that pretty woman with the big afro. Her reflection was in the window.

". . . has always been . . ."

She said again. But I just stood there looking into an empty window until the bus driver asked me if I recognized my own house or not. Walking into my house, the words "stalked by death" was all I was thinking to myself. But I wasn't by myself. Mr. Solomon was there waiting.

"There are roadblocks in front of you, Terrell. Freedom isn't just about leaving prison or the Juvenile Detention Center. It is more about freeing yourself to become a new self, a better self. It's a road to greatness, Terrell. Many of our footprints are on the starting line but few footprints ever cross the finish line."

"The road is that tough?" I asked.

"It can be the most difficult road to travel."

"So tell me what to do."

"Renew your mind, Terrell. Think different and become different. Your road to freedom and greatness begins with your mind. Taking that mental voyage first will make the physical trip that much easier."

I still didn't know how Mr. Solomon knew what was in my head but the more he talked, the more I listened. Listening was a new thing for me, as new as the voices were. I even stopped thinking of what my next response would be, I just listened.

CHAPTER FOURTEEN

"If you don't like something, change it. If you can't change it, change your attitude. Don't complain,"

—Maya Angelou

THE NEXT DAY, I was still thinking of the road to greatness and the traps and obstacles Mr. Solomon was talking about. Avoiding as many of those traps as I could became my goal, but I couldn't avoid them all.

"I heard Mr. Hail gave you a little writing project, Terrell. What is it called, the Juvenile diaries or something? You going to talk about bunk beds and taking group showers or what?"

Most people who had something smart to say would usually say it and keep it moving but our newly elected class leader, Andre Oaks, liked to wait for a response. I didn't like Andre. So talking wasn't what I wanted to do but before I stepped to him, I thought about what I was stepping off of—that road to greatness.

"Few footprints had ever crossed the finish line," was what Mr. Solomon said, and as much as I wanted to finish off Andre, the other finish was becoming more important to me.

"Why are you just standing there looking at your feet?" he said. "Are you afraid of something?"

I guess I was too afraid. Mr. Solomon said thinking different is to be different, but there I was ready fight. It scared me how I could have all the tools to succeed and become provoked to throw it all way. With that in mind, standing there staring at my feet became the responsible choice. That was until one of Andre's friends pushed me against the trophy case I was standing in front of. The glass case didn't shatter, only my self-control did.

"Let's stop it guys. We're smarter than this!"

Andre, the same Andre that started it, calmed everyone down and broke it up and he did it in front of the entire school. No sooner than the annoying "way to go, class Prez" comments begun, echos of "ohhhh hell" started swimming down the hallway. But I ignored them both. I was too busy thinking about how I got from the road to freedom and greatness to nearly fighting in the hallway—and how quickly it happened.

Andre was the first person I blamed. He was the reason I was still in the hallway, angry at myself, and when I heard Mr. Hail and some other teacher coming around the corner, I was ready to blame him for that, too. But Mr. Hail's voice wasn't the first one I heard.

"If you don't like something, change it. If you can't change it, change your attitude. Don't complain,"

It was an older and wiser voice, one that came five minutes too late. "What's your explanation, Mr. Hayes?" Mr. Hail asked. "I see you standing here without the partner I assigned you."

Before I could own up to being a part of the ruckus, I was rescued by the last person I expected.

"I'm here, Mr. Hail." an out of breath Tawanna said while jogging around the corner.

"Fine, Miss Daniels. So how are you two planning to influence behavior? With the pen, that is."

Tawanna didn't have a backup plan after helping me out. It was my turn to help her.

"With voices," "Voices?" he asked.

I looked at Tawanna but she was looking like rescuing me was a mistake. She didn't know about voices.

"Yes, Mr. Hail. We believe the right words can change almost anything. Everyone in this school has something to say that could help someone else. Maybe even more than just one someone."

"So just let students talk? That's your plan to influence behaviour? I see you two don't actually hear the things you all say to each other."

"It won't be our voices we're using, Mr. Hail. I know we all haven't developed the maturity to express ourselves the right way all the time, but there are those in the past like MLK, Maya Angelou, and others that do have the right words for us."

"Voices from the past you say?"

"Voices for choices," I responded with a big smile." "Voices for choices?"

"Yes, sir. We're using the voices of past African American leaders to influence the choices of people our age today."

"Well, I'm curious enough. I'll admit that. Show me what you have soon. And I mean very soon."

Seeing Mr. Hail walking away usually meant I was out of trouble but the real heat I was feeling was coming from somewhere else.

"This is what I stepped in for, so you could add some more craziness to my life? Telling him that we're using students to help students is one thing. But now you're talking about using the voices of dead people? I'm not the ghost whisperer, Terrell! I aint got no African American Ouija board in my wall locker. You don't...do you? We aint the ghost busters, Terrell."

Tawanna was getting warmer but I couldn't tell her about the reflections in the mirrors or the voices, not without making her really freak out. I needed to see Mr. Solomon first. He knew where the voices were coming from. When lunch period came around, I spent most of it thinking of how to get the information I needed from Mr. Solomon. He liked to make me research my own stuff all the time and I didn't feel like doing extra homework. But in our next period, I got distracted from the Mr. Solomon problem by another familiar problem.

"If you want me to wear something else then you start buying my clothes, bitch!"

I'd heard something similar in class before but turning over the table before storming out was a new twist. Our dress code wasn't popular, especially to the girls. Sending students to Mr. Hail's office over leggings and cut off shorts was a regular thing, but by the way Latanya Smalls had acted, I wasn't expecting to see her again that day.

"It's all good though," said one of the other classmates.

"Yep, when she comes back, she'll be wearing the same thing.

Teachers don't run the way we dress," another student said.

I thought about one of the first voices I heard. It was talking about making sure I was ultimately responsible for myself and fighting battles I felt were important. I realized then the battle over sagging jeans wasn't the most important stand to take. It allowed me to focus on more things. And I was willing to bet Latanya had more important things to focus on besides the cuts in her jeans.

"Hey, T, we just got our first project," I said. "What, as table guards?"

"No, Latanya. Let's talk to her about this."

"When, next year? That chic won't be back anytime soon." "She will if we say the right words to Mr. Hail."

"You and these words, boy. Look, we're not school counselors, Terrell."

Tawanna was right but who told the very first counselor he or she was qualified to counsel, I thought. No one—somebody had to start by giving the best advice they could. Tawanna and I had Mr. Hail behind us, so using his name to speak with Latanya was the plan. Latanya didn't like that plan.

"I don't need to speak to them; they're just students like me," she told the ISS teacher.

"She's right," Tawanna whispered. "I wouldn't talk to us either." But eventually Latanya came out into the hallway.

"Okay . . . so?" she said.

I knew Tawanna wasn't going to kick it off so I did, or at least I started to.

"Before you waste your time. I've already called my mom. She's on her way to curse out that teacher, Mr. Hail, and whoever else. Don't get added to the list, alright?"

As the door closed behind her. Suddenly I remembered why my aunt hated us teenagers so much.

"Satisfied? Mr. Hail Jr?"

"Funny," I said to Tawanna, "but what if we could've gotten her to go back to second period and apologize before her mom got here?"

"You really want that Nobel Peace Prize, don't you?"

"Shut up, Tawanna."

Her jokes were getting old. But as soon as we reached the cafeteria for lunch, we saw behavior that was even older and definitely outdated. "Is that wack Alex eating at the big boy table again?" one of three seniors said to one of their classmates. "He just don't get it."

"Yeah, but he's about to."

Alex Stewart was an upperclassman but only because of his age. He wasn't like the rest of them. Alex was hardly like any of us except Brian. His dad made sure of it. He made sure of a lot of things. Alex didn't sag his pants, he didn't use the language we used, he didn't even think like we did.

It was like the voices were speaking to him already, but they weren't. His dad was. But Alex's dad was doing more than just speaking. He was involved in ways most of our moms weren't. Some of us thought his dad was a substitute teacher because he was around so much. That would've been better for Alex if his dad was a substitute teacher.

Sports, clothes, girls, and cars were the common reasons for the haters to hate on each other; having both parents at home became a new one. Having married parents was like shopping at Target, and shopping at Target makes you a target—your way of threatening the fancy or bougie students. Most of our moms could only afford shopping at Walmart, Target was considered better. And being better got you worse around here, Alex had gotten used to that."

"Don't you guys have something better to do," he said "like pulling up your pants or neatly tucking in your shirts for a change. We have dress codes you know."

"Why don't we neatly tuck you into that trash can? Finally get you to shut up for a change."

Alex was so proper it could aggravate anyone. So, it was no surprise to see him ganged up on. I could've easily been one of the boys getting ready to rough up his perfectly tucked sweater vest. But that was me, not Tawanna; she hated bullying. Even in middle school, she made sure anyone who picked on the easier target during dodge ball would pay for it. When she looked at those boys in the cafeteria and said, "I'm sick of this foul stuff," I knew what was about to happen.

"Tawanna, don't you remember what happened last time you tried breaking up something? And where we almost ended up?"

"Since when are you worried about ISS? Wasn't that you last year bragging about winning the ISS perfect attendance award?"

"Since when was the last time someone trusted us enough to put us in charge of anything? ISS isn't going anywhere, Tawanna, but our opportunities might be if we keep doing the same thing."

"So what, Terrell, you want me to draw it instead of doing something about it? Yeah, that's what we should do. I'll just draw how things are supposed to look."

"Yeah, and show it to these guys later. You know, paint a different picture for'em."

"I was kidding, Terrell. You trying to get us beat up, aren't you?"
"The goal is to get us lifted up. How long are we supposed to be down?" I hated how much I sounded like Mr. Solomon. But I really was becoming a product of my new environment. Then my old environment had something to say.

Mirrors

"Is that Terrell over there? How do you go from convict to teacher's pet?" one of them said. And he wasn't alone.

"So lame. Walking around here with a clipboard. Like he's the new school reporter."

"Or school snitch. What does Mr. Hail call his little pets, the Penned Losers?" another joined in.

"Na the Penned Idiots. Check it out.

"You use to be the king of ISS,"
Now you're just the school's pest,
Talking about influencing behavior,
Who has time for that mess,

All we do is get high, get girls, and get money, you're not even getting extra credit for this shit, so who's the real dummy?

So we don't need a school conscience or your school spirit If it aint about being fleek, we aint trying to hear it.
So mind your business or else you'll feel it
Nobody's trying to hear anything from
Mr. Hail's Penned Idiots"

When he was done, all eyes were then on me and I wasn't good with words like that. But fortunately somebody was and she remembered at the perfect time.

"Penned Idiots, Na we're the Penned Influence
And there's no limit to my pen's influence
Lyrics long lasting, outlast any rapper's endurance

To include you weight lifting geeks
Who pretend to be fleek
With the ebonics that you speak

107

So learn proper English before you yell and holla
Instead of standing over Alex, messing with his collar,
Try standing on good character, you just might look taller

As us for us, we're not Mr. Hails pets, we're more like his weapons
Our words are like landmines, so watch where you're stepping
Instead of your chin, it's your character that we're checking
So if a fight is what you want, this is the fight that you're getting."

But that wasn't the kind of fight they were looking for, and by the time everyone in the cafeteria was finished rooting for Tawanna, one of them was having a change of heart.

CHAPTER FIFTEEN

"The need for change has bulldozed a road down
the center of my mind."

—*Maya Angelou*

DEMETRIUS REED WASN'T the one rapping against Tawanna but, he was standing with them. Until we gave him something else to stand for.

"This (rapping) isn't all we do. We're going to change the world," Demetrius just stood there. The boys he was with stood there, too, but not quietly.

"What world are y'all changing? This is only a cafeteria, so relax." was what one of Demetrius's friends said to Tawanna. But Demetrius was tired of relaxing, he was ready to be a part of something.

Tawanna and I nodded but Demetrius's friends shook their heads and walked away.

"I didn't know you could flow like that," he said to Tawanna. And he wasn't alone. Most of them didn't know Tawanna had skills like that. Her brother was what they called a battle-rapper and she used to spar with him for fun. That was years ago, but it sure started looking like she was having fun again.

"I just haven't wanted to in a long time." she said. "But Terrell and I are doing something new. We need other people doing it with us if you ain't scared."

"Scared of what?" Demetrius asked.

That's when I heard . . .

"We know the road to freedom has always been stalked by death."

This time she wasn't talking about a road leading to greatness. It became about Demetrius and the road he was now on. It would lead him away from the people he was used to. I knew it wouldn't be easy for him. He knew it, too.

"Changing changes a lot of other things, especially how people treat you. But I guess you already know what that feels like." he said to me. He was right. We had that in common already.

But Demetrius was more out there, more into the streets than me and Tawanna. Climbing out was going to be harder for him than for some others.

"It's all good. Just let me know what you need from me," he said. "Cool, we'll get with you after school and . . ."

Before I could finish my sentence, Tawanna had other ideas. "Why wait? What this thing needs is an Influence Board, something people can see when they're coming and going."

"Like a billboard advertisement?" Demetrius asked.

"Exactly, but we're advertising a better way to treat each other. If people read better and see better, we might do better."

While Tawanna and Demetrius were strategizing how to implant a moral compass into our jungle of a school, I was amazed at how fast everything was moving. I still wasn't sure how Demetrius was going to deal with some of his friends. It was different for him than it was for me. Other than my attitude, I didn't bring much from Juvi with me to high school. Demetrius brought a whole lot, including the attention of every security guard monitoring our hallways.

When most of us got released from Juvi, the judge promised our juvenile records wouldn't follow us. The judge couldn't do anything about rumors though. Selling drugs put Demetrius in Juvie and I figured that no matter what good we could do, he'll always be seen as a drug dealer.

"Are you good?" he asked me. "Yeah, man. Let's get to work." I said.

"You sure? You look a little iffy about me joining your project." "Not after what I just heard. You and Tawanna could just battle (rap battle) people into changing their ways."

"Flowing is alright but it can't be just about that, right? I'm good at rapping but everybody who was in here is good at something—except being good. So, do think I can help you two with that part?"

"Sure," I said. But I wasn't sure at all. I've heard Solomon talk about identities and how important they can be to us. And Demetrius was one of those students who really seemed to be about that life. He identified with guys in the street, but maybe too much, I thought. I don't think he could tell what I was thinking but it was obvious Tawanna could. By the sideways look she was giving me, (as though I was trying to break up her new rap duo) I could tell what she was thinking. But before any of us would say another word, I heard the right words.

"The need for change has bulldozed a road down the center of my mind."

Then she said it again.

"The need for change has bulldozed a road down the center of my mind."

When I was doing my community service at the JDC, the only interesting thing to see while painting parking lot lines was watching this old man drive his bulldozer through one of our abandoned housing projects. We all used to trip on how no matter what was in front of his bulldozer, he wouldn't stop. It was sometimes metal, iron, bathtubs, it didn't matter. Whatever was keeping the landscape from changing would be demolished. Demetrius wanted his landscape to change, and I learned better than to stand in front a bulldozer.

When I first felt the need to change, I wanted to become the class leader. But changing wasn't my biggest motivation. I just wanted to be seen as somebody. My need wasn't great enough or real enough. Demetrius had a real desire to change, I owed it to him to recognize it. "One thing about us, Demetrius, is that we didn't have to convince Mr. Hail of anything before he trusted us with this. So, you definitely don't have to convince me," I said.

"We just need to convince everyone else," Tawanna said.

"We need to show them what change can do and what it can bring."

All three of us believe that our attitudes and behaviors cost us something. Big or small, it's cost us something. Not allowing negative influences to cost us anything became the new mission.

"Nobody's really different here besides you two. No one really sees a reason to be different, but you two ain't like the rest of us. Why else would Mr. Hail pick you two for this gig?"

"I don't know," I answered

"Probably because we didn't have a choice," Tawanna said.

"Or probably because you made the right choices. I've always said no when someone wanted me to do something different. It was 'no' to Mr. Hail when he always interrupted our dice games in the hallways, 'no' to my mom when she told me to take life more seriously. I've been saying 'no' to change my whole life."

Demetrius wasn't saying 'no' anymore. That was obvious. As obvious as his emotions. None of us were about to cry over anything in high school, but tears weren't necessary to feel ashamed.

"The beginning of my freshman year Mr. Hail told a group of us something serious. 'These next four years will determine your next forty years,' he said. He was looking out. I knew he was. Still, I spent mine like I had another four years coming."

"It's not over, Demetrius. You, me, all three of us are just getting started . . ."

As Tawanna kept talking, the cafeteria suddenly became dark. Not like a "somebody didn't pay the electricity bill" kind of dark, more like the sun was going down. Tawanna kept at her motivational speech and Demetrius kept listening. So once again, I was the only crazy person seeing things. Then I started seeing more than darkness, more than Demetrius and Tawanna. The wall behind them was opening up into something that looked like an old stage or platform.

A very serious looking man was talking to a large crowd of people.

"We should not permit our grievances to overshadow our opportunity," is what he said over and over again. And the people weren't shouting or even talking. None of them were. They were just nodding their heads 'yes' and everyone else looked to be crying.

But a crowd of men crying wasn't what stuck out the most. Seeing so many Black men standing and listening to someone talk was what had me. I never saw that in real life, that kind of respect. It stuck with me. What the man said next stuck with me even more.

"Let us keep before us the fact that, almost without exception, every race or nation that has ever got upon its feet has done so through struggle and trial and persecution; and out of this very resistance to wrong, out of the struggle against odds, they have gained strength, self-confidence, and experience which they could not have gained in any other way."

"Almost without exception," he said. That meant we shouldn't count on being the exception. We have to count on ourselves instead. That's a fact he wanted every one of the men he was addressing to understand. The vision was definitely from an older time when people said we really had a lot to overcome, but they overcame. I knew the vision came to me for my sake, Tawanna, and Demetrius. The easy way wasn't going to be our way, and that's a benefit. One that we didn't see at first.

CHAPTER SIXTEEN

Mr. Washington's lessons

MY AUNT CALLED it feeling "too entitled." She thought we didn't want to work for what we want the way she did. But I was starting to see it another way. I was starting to see that we just didn't know what we were up against, what we're still up against. About a month earlier, a basketball game that I was watching was interrupted with,

"There is a sluggishness, intellectual and academic sluggishness in almost every black community. It's not entirely your fault. The system was (is) designed to make you lose interest in education almost before you were old enough to go to school." But now you must resist all distractions. You must compete academically as though you're competing athletically."

That man's voice was different than the one in my vision but both were saying the same thing.

I rejoined Tawanna's and Demetrius' conversation before they noticed me staring at the wall, but I never stopped thinking about what the man was saying. And why he was saying it. Mr. Solomon always tried making me understand that "learning the why of something prepares us for the next something," so that's what I tried to do.

I remembered as much as I could and googled the words to find out who the man in my vision was. His name was Booker T. Washington. Booker T. Washington was a teacher born in the 1850s. He was also a writer and political advisor. He also founded the college my aunt always bragged about graduating from, Tuskegee University. But before the college and everything, in the 1850s, most of us were slaves—including Booker T. Washington. He carried bags of sawmill to the nearby plantations, bags that weighed as much as he did. But Mr. Washington suffered something even worse than that, something even worse than the beatings he received for not doing his slave chores fast enough. He suffered from a desire to learn.

He used to carry those bags of sawmill across the window of white classrooms every day. Seeing kids his age earning knowledge that would've earned him a beating bothered Booker T. Washington in ways I couldn't understand. After the Civil War he and his mom moved somewhere where he was allowed to learn without being punished; but school would only become his part time job. So waking up at 4 am to study became his routine because he had to work during the day.

But when Booker T. Washington was almost my age, he started working for a coal miner. The coal miner wasn't friendly, but Booker T. Washington didn't need him to be. He just needed him to see. To see that he wasn't like his other workers. He was smart and honest and he didn't cut corners. That kind of stuff impressed the coal miner so much that he allowed Mr. Washington to go to school an hour during work hours each day. An hour didn't seem like much to me until I started thinking how much time an hour is when you use every minute of it.

Booker T. Washington never stopped working for his education. When he was almost twenty, he walked and worked his way to Hampton, Virginia (where I live now). Overall it was almost 500 miles. He couldn't pay for school but they let him work as a janitor to pay for tuition. The school's founder, a man named General Samuel Armstrong, became Mr. Washington's mentor. Maybe Mr. Samuel Armstrong saw Booker T's feet after walking 500 miles and wondered what all he could do with a little help. The man did help Booker T. Washington. After graduating and teaching in Hampton, Booker T. Washington was recommended to run Tuskegee University in Alabama. After that success, he became the first Black advisor to the president—President Theodore Roosevelt.

Booker T. Washington never asked for anything. He never expected anything. He just said, 'watch me work'. And every time someone watched him work with the little he had, they gave him more tools to work with. Eventually they gave Mr. Washington an entire college to work with. I read that a lot of blacks didn't like Mr. Washington because he didn't seem to fight racism enough. I don't know if he didn't wear t-shirts or carry signs or whatever. But he definitely fought racism. Just instead of asking for God-given equality, he taught blacks to earn what was supposed to be free. I know that was unpopular then because it still is now. My mom and I still hate buying bottled water because that used to be free, but we definitely value those bottles of water more than those free cups of tap.

Mr. Washington said many things to me before I even knew who he was. I guess he got tired of seeing me always looking for tap water. He became another teacher to me. He started out teaching blacks from his time with his sweat and hard work, and ended up teaching the entire country. I read these words from him.

"There are two ways of exerting one's strength: one is pushing down, the other is pulling up."

That didn't make much sense the first time I read it, but I screen-saved it. The second time was in Gym class. We were having a push-up and pull-contest to see who all got a free gym day or who didn't. Over twenty of us volunteered for the pushups and maybe two or three for the pullups. Then I heard him actually say it.

"There are two ways of exerting one's strength: one is pushing down, the other is pulling up."

It was right as the contest started. We were yelling and talking trash back and forth, and when it was over, Mr. Washington's words became easier to understand. The pushups and pull up exercises were symbolic to something bigger: pushing yourself away from one thing, pulling yourself over something else. Everyone in class did more pushups. Pushing was so much easier, but my gym teacher emphasized the more difficult exercise.

"Work on your pull ups," she said. "Pulling your own body weight may help you pull someone else's one day."

Mr. Washington was talking about the same thing. I could see how much easier it was to separate ourselves from what's underneath than to pull what's underneath up. Understanding that made me want to understand even more.

I started thinking about the other voices I heard and what they meant but getting caught trying to Google them in the hallway wasn't a punishment I could afford. Especially after finding out we were finally on Mr. Hail's good side.

"There you are," Tawanna yelled from the down the hall. "That sentence you wrote on the Penned Influence Board must've meant something to somebody. Mr. Hail moved the board from the main office to the cafeteria. Now everybody will see our work, not just the ones going to ISS."

Tawanna wasn't lying. When we walked down to the cafeteria, there it was on a huge dry erase board.

"I have learned that success is to be measured not so much by the position that one has reached in life as by the obstacles which he

has had to overcome while trying to succeed."—Booker T. Washington

When I first scribbled those words on the information board outside of Mr. Hail's office, he grilled me about where I heard them from. I knew I couldn't tell him that a voice came to me while I was reading about the rich and famous rappers in a Hip-hop magazine, but I didn't want to lie either. So I came up with the best response I could think of.

"I was reading about the fancy lifestyles of ball players and rappers. It's easy to see why we want their lifestyles. But then I started thinking about our project and if the messages from the magazine were the right kind of influences we need."

"So, are they?" he asked.

"I thought so at first but the pictures in the magazine don't tell the whole story. Pictures of jewelry, girls, and cars don't motivate me to out-hustle someone in the classroom. Instead, they motivate me to out-hustle someone in the street or on the court. We're trying to hustle academically as though we're hustling athletically."

"And what of the quote you wrote on my board?"

"Yeah, I was looking up what success really is and I came across that quote by Booker T. Washington."

"Well, good job, Terrell. I'm going to leave it up for a while." He didn't just leave it up, he added something to it.

At that point I wasn't embarrassed anymore. I was proud of it. Seeing those words framed at the entrance of the school, I thought the whole thing was awesome. Tawanna and Demetrius had the same facial expressions I had. The experience of overcoming what our peers said about this project reminded me of a rap verse of Jay Z my brother used to always repeat,

"I'm not afraid of dying, I'm afraid of not trying, Everyday hit every wave like I'm Hawaiian."

Andrew D Shepherd

We weren't Hawaiian, and we didn't live on the beach, but waves in concrete can rise just as high as water and drown you just as quickly. And even while some students continued talking, snickering, and debating our message boards, I still wanted to research some of the other things those people were telling me. Everything they told me helped, and I knew it could help others, too. But history class was coming up and I knew better than to pull out my phone to look them up. In some classrooms, it was dangerous to even stick your hands in your pockets for too long.

Walking in and seeing that Mrs. Hatley had finished our lesson on the Industrial Revolution, I was hoping to learn about something interesting like the Harlem Renaissance. But that wasn't about to happen. Mrs. Hatley put up a large map of Gettysburg, Pennsylvania and said "this is why we're all here together now".

She went on to teach how the battle at Gettysburg won the Civil War and that along with the Thirteenth Amendment, won freedom for slaves. Eventually, slaves became Martin Luther King. In elementary school, I heard something similar; but then all I cared about was ignoring everything until recess began. It was different now. After learning about men like Booker T. Washington, I wanted the whole story. So what I did was once unthinkable. I raised my hand.

"Yes, Terrell, you can have a bathroom pass," she immediately said. But I couldn't get mad. My history in History class gave that impression.

"No ma'am, I just have a question. What other historic African Americans were there? I'm saying, Martin Luther King can't be it."

Especially with all the different people guiding me. But then her reply let me know what was guiding her.

"Well, I'm sure there were many African American's who contributed to this nation, but we only learn about those who made such an impact as he."

"What do you mean?" I asked.

"Martin Luther King helped change this country, Terrell. We all must learn about him."

"But it had to have been more people, too, right? He must've seen what others did and took it further, right? Like in sports, before Lebron there was Kobe and before Kobe there was Michael Jordan and before Michael Jordan there were others, too, I bet."

"It was Doctor J," said one of the other students. "Mr. Lewis (the Junior Varsity Basketball Coach) keeps bringing him up whenever he tries teaching us the players we should emulate on the court."

"That's very nice everyone," said an increasingly irritated Mrs. Hatley," but we're not talking about games.

"But ma'am, in the game of life, shouldn't we learn who we should emulate? I bet there were African Americans that Martin Luther King learned from. I know you said Martin Luther King followed the teachings of Mahatma Gandhi, but there were a lot African Americans around during that time who did some pretty amazing stuff."

"*We must reinforce argument with results,*" someone said. But it wasn't Mrs. Hatley. It was Booker T. Washington's voice. He heard me giving Mrs. Hatley my opinion without having other examples to back them up with. But I wasn't the only one with something to say.

"Mrs. Hatley, let you tell it, running and jumping around on the plantation fields and sports fields are all we're good at. It's really not."

"I'm sure I wasn't saying that at all, Jaden. Just like I'm sure you all know that we teachers don't decide the curriculum . . ."

While Mrs. Hatly continued telling us the ins and outs of student curriculums, the same words were repeated to me but with a different meaning.

"We must reinforce argument with results."

But this time he was telling me to not just find other examples in history of African American men and women, but to also see how learning about them could potentially put them into a teaching curriculum.

The first step I took was just a baby step, but even that was in the wrong direction.

"You want to do what!" Tawanna said.

"I think he wants to have some kind of lunch room black history class." said Demetrius.

"Guys, our thing is called Penned Influences so let's write about what African Americans did that can still influence others. It makes perfect sense."

"Yeah, Terrell, WRITE about it," Tawanna said in her not-so polite voice. "Not teach it. Who are we supposed to be? School jokers are who we'll end up being if we start reciting Martin Luther King's" I Have A Dream" speech while people are trying to eat their chicken tenders."

"You see, guys, that's my point. MLK is all we know."

"Terrell, RIP is all you'll know if you try to turn this into some cafeteria teaching class. I'm serious."

As serious as Tawanna's and Demetrius' words were, the other words had more influence over me at that point. So, when that day ended, my black history plans did not. When the bus arrived at my house, I saw Mr. Solomon's car parked outside. I knew he would have some advice for me, but when I walked into the house, he was giving some other kind of advice—the kind that changed everything.

CHAPTER SEVENTEEN

Pains and Gains

I WOULD USUALLY WALK into the door hearing them in the kitchen talking about my progress, but that day mom and Solomon were upstairs in Malik's room talking.

"This isn't a new idea, Solomon. Don't you think I've considered this? Ever since Malik was sent to that place, and every time we visited him, he and Terrell smiled through that glass as if we were at a water park instead of a prison."

"Children today have been fooled into believing that there are worse things than prisons."

"I'm only concerned with my two boys, Solomon. And you're here telling me to not let one of them come home."

That's when I realized what they were discussing. They were talking about Malik coming home. But Mr. Solomon was saying . . .

"I'm here asking you to consider letting one make his own way. In my village we called it 'Ukuvula Umnyango Kusaba Khona,' To Open The Door No More. This saying told us boys the revolving door was closing and we must hang our hinges elsewhere."

"And you want me to tell my firstborn child to hang his hinges on a navy ship? I'm a widow because of that military, Solomon. Sending another one of my men into the service—you're asking too much."

"I'm not asking for myself."

Despite his reasons, the only thing I understood was that my mentor was trying to break apart my family. And I couldn't keep quiet.

"Mom! Malik is coming home?" "Yes, Terrell. He's getting released."

"That means he's coming home, right?"

They both just looked at me as if they didn't want me in the conversation. But I needed to know what answer my mom was going to give. Then she gave it the same way she gave every other answer when it came to Malik—she started taking things off his walls. It only took a few more minutes for her to erase any evidence that Malik lived with us. Besides his bags she packed for me to carry downstairs, it looked as if Malik never lived with us at all.

"I'm good," I said to Solomon as he tried to help me carry them.

He'd already helped enough in my opinion.

"You're really doing this, mom? You're sending him away before even knowing he's going to get in trouble again," I said after returning from downstairs.

"This is for Malik, Terrell. He needs a different environment. Getting released amongst the same people is only going to put him in the same situations. And send him the same place again. By now you understand this, Terrell."

"But he's getting released to us, Mom—to his family."

It didn't matter what I said, she just kept handing me more bags.

And Solomon didn't care about what I said either because he kept trying to help me with those bags.

"I said I don't need any help," I finally told him.

"You better watch your mouth, young man," was the next thing I heard.

"Mom, I'm trying to carry all this stuff but he . . ."

"He's what, Terrell? He's asking if you need help! You're lucky someone's here helping you at all, so help yourself downstairs."

No matter how much I tried to avoid Solomon, he was still there—trying to help. But it still wasn't the help I was looking for.

124

"The recruiter will meet him at the prisoner release point. I've explained everything to him."

"Thank you, Solomon."

"I know this isn't easy. We all will get through." Solomon said.

But I couldn't believe what I was hearing. That's probably why the next thing I said was something I couldn't believe either.

"We?" while snatching the bag from his hand. "Man you aint in this with us! You're not a part of this family! You should get back on your damn zebra and roll back to Africa."

I felt it as soon as I said it, that bad feeling on the inside when you know you've messed up. The feeling got worse when I looked down the stairs and saw the clothes fall out of the bag after I snatched it. I couldn't look right at Solomon after saying that and I definitely wasn't going to look at my mom—and they knew it.

Solomon carried the last bag downstairs and my mom followed him. After that, they sat at the dinner table and ate. I went to bed hungry that night. The next morning, I didn't see my mom before the bus came. I did my best to make sure of that.

Though I was out of character the night before, everyone was playing their normal roles at school the next day.

"FAD is going to be crazy. They've been waiting all year to show me what they got for me," said a student in the hallway.

"For you? The Free Attire Day is just another way for the girls to show how much I mean to them. Being caged in those lame uniforms for so long should have them itching to bust out into something more." "Or something less," another said as the three of them laughed on the bus ride to school. That kind of conversation was common on Free Attire Day. The guys liked wearing all the stuff that was off limits to us but we really couldn't wait to see what the girls wore. Most times it was like we were seeing new students, by how different some of them looked without the rule book holding them back.

"Good look, Sugarfoot" was the first thing I remember hearing when I walked into school. The girl who it was said to turned and smirked at the boy saying it. That was probably the only "G" rated thing said that day. But no matter what the girls wore, it was too much clothing for us. Even the outfits that use to get girls sent to Mr. Hail's office wasn't enough on FAD, I guess that's why FAD was the one day a semester Mr. Hail took a day off. The teachers would say he was sick. If he saw the behavior in his absence, it would've given him the flu.

"I'm saying, Teresa. We did the same thing last year." "That was last year, Shaun."

"Exactly. So as upperclassmen we should be stepping our game up, right?"

I walked up on this conversation going on beside the outside vending machines. We always said that "pressure bust pipes," but this dude was trying to bust the whole kitchen.

"Stop playing, T. The bell just rung so we got a good minute before anyone's out here.'"

"That's what you said last time and one of boys had me doing stuff on his phone, Shaun."

"I told you, I made him erase all of that."

I didn't know Shaun but I might as well had known him. We all might not have been cut from the same cloth, but when it came to how we engaged girls, most of our minds were in the same mud. "Poisoning our own crops" was what Mr. Solomon called it.

I was remembering Mr. Solomon's words clear as day that morning, but I could hear Shaun and Teresa, too; and it was obvious that sort of thing wasn't new to them. But then I finally heard something that was new to me.

"Just because somebody's ok with it doesn't make it ok."

But that time it wasn't Booker T. Washington, Arthur Ashe, or anyone else. It was my own inner voice talking to me. And I knew there wasn't much time between the two bells and even less time for Teresa. As I walked back toward where she and Shaun were at, I began to think about what I was actually doing. The right thing aside, it began to feel like a bad idea. But the closer I got, the more I heard Shaun convincing Teresa of an even worse idea.

"I must be tripping," I thought. And that's when it happened.

"Are you stupid, man? What are you doing back here? Your clumsy ass tripped all over us."

"I was ummm . . ." Before I could think of a reason of being back there, Teresa started buttoning her shirt and running away at the same time. So I guess it's mission complete, I thought to myself. Although slipping off a step and getting grass stains on my jeans weren't a part of the mission.

"You did this on purpose didn't you?" Shaun asked. "Yeah, you're one of Mr. Hail's Penned Pecker Heads."

Penned Pecker Heads? Whatever happened to Penned Idiots, I could at least defend against that one. But seeing the way Shaun started looking at me, I knew that I had to be ready to defend against more than just words. At least I thought I did.

"Terrell, man we got work to do. What are you doing out here? How you get grass stains on your jeans. You know your mama only buy you one pair a semester . . ." But before Demetrius could finish his joke and Tawanna could get her laugh out, they both noticed my fists were balled and Shaun's were, too.

"What's up, Shaun," Demetrius said in a way that made Shaun reconsider his next move.

"It ain't nothing. We good," Shaun replied. And that was good enough for me. I was satisfied with interrupting Teresa from agreeing to do something she didn't want to do anymore. That situation gave me a new quote for our Penned Influences board.

"Associate yourself with people of good quality, for it is better to be alone than in bad company."

"No one can degrade us except ourselves."

Booker T. Washington said these two things to me about a month before that thing with Shaun and Teresa. I was watching a TV special on Karrine Steffans, AKA Superhead. I was listening to what rap stars and athletes were saying about her but I didn't know Solomon was behind my chair watching and listening as well.

"Another Superhead is invented every Friday and Saturday night," he said. "Probably not to that extent, but the seeds are certainly planted."

"How?" I asked.

"Men plant seeds everyday with no intentions to water or nurture them, but we pretend to be surprised when those seeds grow into weeds of resentment. It's much like the card games your mother and aunts play. Everyone is so careful to win without reneging because once trust is gone, it's nearly impossible to recover. But we men, young and old, are drowning in the belief that reneging is winning and that cheating and lying are ok. This is no good, Terrell."

I never heard a guy claim responsibility for how women turn out, especially the guys I grew up hearing. People at school weren't used to hearing it either.

"No one can degrade us except ourselves"

"Are you three from the Hallmark channel or what?" was what one upperclassman said. Then her boyfriend added,
"Naw, look at the rest of it."

'Associate yourself with people of good quality, for it is better to be alone than in bad company.'

"Yo . . . this the virgin diaries."

Those two got a pretty big laugh inside the cafeteria but it wasn't too hard ignoring them. For me, it was ignoring some of the other students that became the harder job. Students like Alisha Kay. Alisha was Mr. Hail's niece and I wished she would've taken a sick day alongside her uncle. Our imaginations of how some of the students looked in regular clothes were all most of us had to go on in a school with uniforms and dress codes. Alisha Kay made all of us imagine the most.

When she walked into the cafeteria with her friends, the chocolate milks got warm, the chicken sandwiches got cold, and no one was interested in sports anymore—especially me. All I could think about was hiding that stupid message board before she saw what some of the others were laughing at.

"Ouch!" I said after being pinched by Tawanna's plier-like fingers. "I'm just waking you up from your day-dream."

"I wasn't daydreaming."

"Boy, bye. You're just like the rest of these porn-zombies when she comes around."

"Porn-zombie? Really, Tawanna?"

"Whatever. You just be ready to explain this message to her if she walks over here."

"You being a girl, don't you think you should?"

"It's your message, Terrell. Stop being a punk. OMG, boy, are you sweating?"

"If I am it's because of your blazing breath. So, leave me alone." But the truth was I had never been more nervous. I was more comfortable in front of the judge who sent me to the JDC. I guess if the judge looked like Alisha Kay, I would've melted away there, too. Luckily, Alisha walked the opposite way before the questions came.

"So yall just writing about the way we do each other or what?" someone asked. Before Demetrius could answer, another student gave his own answer.

"Naw cuz, they're talking about the 'N' word. My moms be kicking the same spill. Stop calling each other that and stop dressing like thugs and the cops might stop treating us like thugs, right? Is that what you all mean?"

"Na, Zabian." I answered. "That wasn't what we were thinking when we put it up here, but that doesn't make your moms wrong either."

"It doesn't make her right either," he responded. "How I dress, walk and talk shouldn't have anything to do with how I'm treated."

I wanted to agree with him. I wanted to think presentation didn't matter. But before all this started happening in the cafeteria I bought a chicken sandwich from the line and it took me a minute just to pick out the one that was wrapped neatly and not just thrown together. And that was just choosing a sandwich.

"Are you listening, Terrell? This your board right?"

"Yeah, this is our board, Zabian, and I believe what's written on it. We do degrade ourselves; that's a true statement. I'm not naming names, but I almost tripped over one of us trying to get it in with a girl behind the building this morning. Is that what she's here for? Is that the best we can do? Calling each other the 'N' word, is that the best we can do?"

"Man, you know who you sound like?" Zabian asked.

I didn't answer. I knew exactly who I sounded like. The same person I disrespected a day earlier. But Zabian was thinking about Mr. Hail, not Mr. Solomon.

"You sound just like Mr. Hail. He be calling himself spitting fire at us the same way."

Zabian had a point but it was pointed in the wrong direction. He thought every time an adult spoke to him a way he didn't like meant the adult wasn't on his side. He was wrong about that.

"Maybe Mr. Hail keeps coming at us with fire to keep us out the fire, Z. You ever thought about that?"

Zabian didn't have an answer, but someone else did.

"I've thought about that," one of the upperclassmen girls said from behind the crowd that gathered around us. After she made her way through everyone, I saw who it was.

"Mr. Hail's been preaching to me about the decisions I've made since I was in middle school."

I was hoping Teresa would stop there, but luck is never on my side. "If you didn't come out there this morning, Terrell . . . I would've
had something else to regret.

I didn't know what to say after that. Everybody was looking at me but all I wanted for them to do was to look at the board instead.

"That's a good look on you, Terrell, the hero cape. And you didn't even need this message board to do the right thing, did you?"

"How does anyone know if they will have what it takes to do what's right when that time comes?" I asked

"You did, Terrell. This morning you did," said Tawanna looking at me as if I was better than I thought I was.

"I like what you said. It took courage," said Alisha Kay before following the crowd out of the cafeteria. But Alisha wasn't the last one in the cafeteria. Standing in the back was someone who I didn't expect to see and didn't want to see.

"I guess this is what Mr. Wilks was talking about last semester, Terrell."

"What's that, Mr. Moyer?"

"Your leadership ability. Other than distractions and sidebar conversations during my classes, I've never seen you and Tawanna capable of leading much else."

"Yes, sir. I bet no other teachers did either."

"We don't have a crystal ball hidden away in our classrooms, Terrell. We just have you all. All sixteen hundred of you."

"What does that mean, Mr. Moyer? That it's too many of us to treat fairly?"

"No, but it could mean there's too many of you to second guess. I have to believe what you show me, Terrell. The Terrell you showed everyone the first semester of school is totally different than the Terrell I just heard addressing the cafeteria a few minutes ago."

"People change, Mr. Moyer."

"People do change, Terrell. That's correct. But who said there's always time to change? Whoever said there's always the opportunity? 'In all our deeds, the proper value and respect for time determines success or failure . . . '"

"Wait, who said that? I mean, I know you just did but who said it first?"

"Are you surprised to hear a White man quoting Malcolm X?"

I didn't know who Mr. Moyer was quoting but knew someone said those same words to me before. Just then I knew who it was. At that point I wanted to research the words I've heard even more, while I could still remember them.

"Do you know what he meant by that, Mr. Moyer?"

"Malcolm X meant the time is now, Terrell. The time to grow up, to stop making excuses, and to take your life seriously is always right now. He meant success is now. Not after you're tired of the games, the girls, and the partying, but right now. Words like later, tomorrow, next semester aren't guaranteed, only right now is. And right now, Terrell . . . you're late for the next class. But I can help you with that."

As we both smiled while he wrote me a note for class, I wanted to apologize to Mr. Moyer for hating him so much after overhearing what he said to Mr. Wilks last semester. But I didn't. Teachers like Mr. Moyer, Mr. Wilks, and Mr. Hail didn't want to hear "I'm sorry". They'd rather just see it. After that conversation with Mr. Moyer, he began to see my potential and I began to see the potential for more opportunities.

During the push up contest in gym class, six of us tied at forty-eight, so we all got a free day. The basketball court would've normally been my first stop but Mr. Moyer had me thinking about that quote from Malcolm X and all the others. Forty-eight minutes later, I was surprised with how much I could remember and write down in under an hour; but I still had to research them to find out what they all meant. That's when more opportunities poured in.

"Good afternoon class, I'm Ms. Barry, and I'll be subbing for Mrs. Hatley today. I see you've completed the Industrial Revolution and are now at the Civil War period. Does that sound about right?"

After everyone murmured "yeeesss" Ms. Barry flipped a few more pages of Mrs. Hatley's lesson plan and became even less excited than we were.

"I'll tell you what," she looked up at us and said, "you all spend this hour naming and researching no less than three historical people or events that spurred from the Civil War, and for homework you will write about each and we'll discuss them tomorrow. Agreed?"

"Agreed!" Everyone yelled.

I yelled the loudest (on the inside), because I finally got time to find who's been talking to me for the last semester. But first I wanted to learn about this Malcolm X guy Mr. Moyer was talking about. When I Googled him, two very different descriptions came up like Mr. Solomon described. Some people viewed him a champion for justice and human rights while others called him a racist and radical but I didn't think a white teacher like Mr. Moyer would quote a black racist, so I kept reading. After more research, it was easy to tell why some people called Malcolm a racist. The same people would've call my grandmother a racist, too. I used to hear her and her sisters talk about how things used to be back then.

She didn't complain or blame anyone. I think she used it as motivation to work harder and not expect anything for free. Malcolm X must have looked at things the same way because I found out it was his voice I heard last semester when I was ok with eating chips and watching TV all day.

"Education is the passport to the future, for tomorrow belongs to those who prepare for it today," was what he said to me; and he was right. The more I learned about Malcolm X the more it seemed like I was learning about myself. Like him, I had to learn that being angry wouldn't change anything. We both had to change ourselves first.

He became a minister and I'm doing this Penned Influences thing but it was all the same to me.

The more things I remembered hearing the more people I discovered who were talking to me. It wasn't odd anymore. Especially after finding out who they all were.

Like Arthur Ashe. He talked to me about responsibility and choosing the right battles to fight back when I still thought the right of sagging my pants was something worth holding a picket sign for. Even when I wasn't sure about talking to Mr. Wilks about becoming a class leader, it was Arthur Ashe's voice that said "You've got to get to the stage in life where going for it is more important than winning or losing" and "One important key to success is self-confidence."

He knew I was afraid of trying for something without knowing what the outcome would be. That's the opposite of courage. By being afraid, I was opposing my own potential. He also knew I didn't properly prepare for what I was trying to achieve. Thanks to Mr. Ashe, that won't happen again. Now that I'm learning more about who I am and who I can be, a lot of things won't happen again. Like putting people down. I use to think it was cool to clown people until I heard the truth.

"You can't hold a man down without staying down with him," was something Booker T. Washington told me after I was feeling good at another classmate's expense, which was similar to something Mr. Solomon told me one day when he asked how long my arm was. He measured my arm and said, "That's how far you are from anyone you're trying to hold down or hold back—just a few feet."

After spending the rest of History class writing down all I could remember, the next bell was only a few minutes away. I had just remembered it was a mentoring day. I never apologized to Mr. Solomon and I knew I owed him big. Not for what he did for me, but for what he had been trying to do. A simple "I'm sorry" wasn't going to be enough. Especially after everything I learned today. After all, Mr. Solomon was the only person to understand what was happening. But to really pull it off, I had to do something he wouldn't approve of at first. I had to lie to someone. Emailing Mr. Solomon everything I learned about the historic African Americans was one thing, but being able to print it out and hand it to him with my apology was something much more. I would call it Their Voices, My Choices.

But to make it happen, I needed to print. and no one could print unless it was school business. So, I had to make it school business.

"Mrs. Stevens?" "Yes, Terrell?"

"I finished Mr. Hail's project, but I can only send it to my email. He wants it printed, I think."

"Sure, Terrell. Send it to the school's email and I will print it for you."

"Yes, ma'am. But first, can we fix it up a little bit? I have it on a Word document, but I'd rather have it looking a little fancy before Mr. Hail sees it."

"I'm not a graphic designer, Terrell. I can print it out for you, but that's about it."

"Maybe you can let me sit there for a minute. Just a minute, Mrs. Stevens."

She paused for a few seconds looking me up and down—my old reputation definitely proceeded me. But that day she saw a shirt tucked in, pants pulled up and she heard a few "ma'ams" thrown in there. I realized for the first time what a good presentation could get me.

"Ok, Terrell. Just for a minute."

And a minute was all I needed. About a year before then I was helping my mom format her church's teen devotional handouts, something they were giving to teenagers graduating from high school. They never finished putting it all together but I still had the page layouts on my email. They were perfect.

"Hurry up, Terrell. I have work to do."

"Almost done, Mrs. Stevens. Facebook isn't going anywhere (I said under my breath). But I was almost done. And when it finally printed out, Mrs. Stevens thought it belonged to someone else.

"A thirty-day devotion? Whose class is this for?" she asked everyone in the main office.

"That's mine," I said.

"Terrell, you better print what you need and get out of here."
"Seriously, Mrs. Stevens. Look at the final page."

And there it read, by Terrell Hayes.

I left the office smiling more than usual. It wasn't every day I surprised my mom and Solomon with something positive. But I didn't make it very far down the hallway before I was reminded that everyone doesn't like surprises. The halls are pretty wide in our school, but I guess some students wanted to take up the entire hallway. When Thomas's shoulder hit me, he hit my side that was holding my devotional papers.

"What's this crap?" he said while bending down. "Voices for Choices . . . you're really trying to be a teacher aren't you?"

"Yeah, something like that," I said hoping it would be enough for Thomas to back off. It wasn't enough."

"So this is why my boy changed up on me. Your little project."
"What's your problem?"

"My problem is you're in my business. Hang up another poster. It'll be you getting hung up somewhere."

I didn't know what he meant, and he didn't look to be in an explaining mood. Thomas was what we called a "senior citizen" because he was a senior but looked older than the teachers. Failing two grades will do that, I guess. But I couldn't see what his problem with me was. All I saw were the footprints he left on some of my devotional papers.

"You're lucky those aren't on your face," someone said. "My what?"

"Those footprints on them papers. Thomas is more known for stomping people instead of paper."

"Why are you telling me this?" I asked.

"I'm just doing the humanitarian thing, saving lives and all. I was downtown this weekend. I saw the whole thing. Thomas, Demetrius, everyone. A lot of money got lost since Demetrius got off the streets. A lot of Thomas's money."

"And?"

"And your little Penned Suicides message board is what got Demetrius seeing things differently all of a sudden."

"That's the point."

"Yeah, ok," he said before walking away.

Mirrors

This student just came out of nowhere talking about things I wasn't a part of, or at least I thought I wasn't. That's when I learned the true power of words. How something written or heard could change people in ways you don't see.

CHAPTER EIGHTEEN

Strangers and Aliens

A S SOON AS I got all the devotional papers back together, someone hit my shoulder again, knocking all the papers out my hand again. But this time I wasn't the target. I was just in the way.

"Out back!" "Out back!" was what they all were yelling and the whole school seemed to be following. By the time I picked up my paper and made it outside, it looked like the school was having a concert on the soccer field—everyone was down there. The closer I got, the more it really became a show.

"Get up, Demetrius!" "Fight!"

"Hit'em back!" were the constant chants from everyone. Thomas, being bigger and older, didn't need cheerleaders. He didn't want anyone on his side. Thomas just wanted Demetrius to regret his choice. I wasn't sure how close he got before the security guards broke it up, but Demetrius was still standing when it was over.

"You're nobody now!" Thomas yelled. "You're not even from here anymore," he continued to say until his yells were drowned out by another voice—a familiar voice.

"I had crossed the line. I was free; but there was no one to welcome me to the land of freedom. I was a stranger in a strange land."

It was loud, louder than all the yelling and arguing. She was explaining the line Demetrius had crossed. She was explaining how we might not be welcomed with friendly faces after crossing over to a new place. And everyone isn't going to celebrate your freedom, especially those still imprisoned by their old ways.

But I could see the looks on some of their faces, Demetrius wasn't as alone as he thought he was. Yells of "It's all good man" and "He's not worth it, Demetrius" weren't as loud as the chants encouraging the fight, but I could hear them. So could Demetrius.

I wasn't able to find Demetrius before the buses began leaving so I made sure I remembered the woman's words that time. But I remembered what I was carrying most of all. When the bus arrived at my house, I was ready for Mr. Solomon to see it. But when I walked inside, it wasn't my living room I was walking into. I looked down at my clothes and they were different. The smell was horrible, but it was familiar to me. I was back at the dope house with Phillip. Some how I flashed back there but this time I didn't leave right away. I walked deeper inside with Phillip where his cousin was cutting up drugs. Then I saw Shauna.

"You haven't learned a single thing I taught you, have you? You haven't even learned anything about yourself. I should have enough powder on this table for you to lay down and make snow angels by now, but I don't, do I? All of a sudden my little angel don't like lying down anymore, huh?"

The way she was standing there, it was saddest thing I ever saw. "I ain't doing it no more . . . I can't!

She just kept saying that but Raheem knew her better than she knew herself.

"Nah, you can do anything I need you to do baby. You just gotta believe in yourself."

That's when he noticed Phillip and me.

"Phil, what's up cuz? Get in here. Don't mind us. It takes two people to make up one mind sometimes. But I think it's made up now.

The way she sort of hid in that corner, it looked like he'd been making her mind up for a while now. I didn't think she wanted to be there any more than me or Phillip, whether he would've admitted it or not.

"Is this my new runner?" Raheem asked,

"Yea, this is Terrell but I don't know if he's . . ." Philip answered. "You don't know if he's what, Phil? If he's down? You brought em here . . ."

I definitely wasn't down. Not with any of it. If I knew that cutting class to smoke weed was going to land me there, I never would've done it. But Raheem wasn't trying to hear that.

"Everybody is telling me what they can't do today. Let me tell you what I can't do. I can't be having outsiders knowing the inside of my business. You understand that, don't you? Or do you want to know the insides of something or someone else?"

He kept catching me looking at his girlfriend. He wanted me looking at his girl. Jealousy wasn't Raheem's thing, opportunity was.

"Well don't just stand there."

He was looking directly at me, but I knew he wasn't talking to me.

The way he was grinning almost kept me from noticing her walking my way, or trying to walk.

There shouldn't be any such thing as a broken spirit limit, but I had reached mine.

I'm sure Phillip was laughing or whatever, but it was too much for me. That's when I ran out. I started running so fast it felt like I was running away from something. This time I didn't black out or lose time. I didn't lose anything. I was actually found.

It wasn't dark but it was like they were in the shadows.

"There is in this world no such force as the force of a person determined to rise." When will you finally rise, Terrell?

I didn't need to rise, I thought. I was already up.

"The time is now to rise, Terrell."

When I looked closer at them, it looked like I was looking into an old movie with the way they were dressed and standing. But then it became my movie, with the two of them narrating it. It didn't last long before I started to dislike what I was hearing. At first, their words almost made me dislike who I was. But they weren't interested in who I was, only in who I was meant to be.

"We should not permit our grievances to overshadow our opportunity."

"The Talented Tenth of our race must be made leaders of thought and missionaries of culture among their people. This lifestyle that you've been introduced to, this way of thinking that has apprehended the focus of much of your generation, this isn't our culture Terrell. Consider the energy you just spent running from that culture."

"There are two ways of exerting one's strength: one is pushing down, the other is pulling up."

"But in order to pull someone up, you must be up, Terrell. You must remain up."

I did remain up but I didn't remain in that flashback. The lights that hit me this time weren't Mr. Solomon's headlights, but the flashlight from my sister's smartphone.

I didn't know who Brittany was but I was pretty sure that other girl dancing was my sister. As strange as the sight was, the slight joy I felt was even stranger. I knew enough to know that college wasn't easy and Patricia wouldn't be dancing unless she had something to celebrate. But that joy went as quickly as we made eye contact.

"Boy, what are you doing?" Patricia said in her usual aggravating way.

"What are you two doing?" I asked. Before either could respond, someone else answered with;

"Reality is wrong. Dreams are for real."

I wasn't sure who it was and definitely didn't realize how crazy I was looking while staring in space.

"Girl, what's wrong with your brother?"

"Terrell?"

"Nothing, I'm good. What's this?"

"You don't look good."

That's because I really wasn't good. Not at all. I felt like the whole world was spinning the wrong way.

"Seriously, what's going on with you, Terrell?"

"Study your work, don't be studying me. I told you I'm good."

Patrice knew me. She knew when I was lying. But her friend seemed to only know one thing . . .

"Boy, you need to try studying this," she said while standing up to dance. I've seen my sister and her friends dance many times, usually ending up with one of her girls teasing me—nothing I needed to relive. Then I heard the lyrics they were reciting.

"The more you spend it, the faster it go, Bad bitches, on the floor, its rainin' hunnids Throw some mo', throw some mo'"

When I turned to watch the two of them singing and dancing, it reminded me of a music video I saw earlier that year. Then I started thinking about Tawanna again. After thinking about how she was smiling and flirting with the same guys that were taking advantage of her, I started thinking about why I even cared. It seemed everybody was doing exactly what made them happy. For me, all I wanted to do was go to sleep. I never got what I wanted.

"Reality is wrong. Dreams are for real"

That voice sounded like it came from right outside my door, but it was inside my room. He, Tupac Shakur, was inside my room.

"Listen to me, man. Stop being caught up on what you see in the world and how it's so different from what your Mr. Solomon is trying to teach you."

"It does paint a different picture . . . you even have admit that."

"Have you ever heard the saying 'life imitates art more often than art imitates life'?"

"No, but what does that have to do with anything?"

"Music is art, Terrell. How do you feel about the art you're hearing outside your door? How would you feel if your sister's life began to imitate that art?"

"You mean like Tawanna's life beginning to. She used to be all about poetry and spoken word until we got her listening to our junk. She almost became junk."

"There is no almost. Tawanna is becoming the warrior princess she's destined to be. All of them will, in some way. Some are just slipping from their throne is all. Didn't Brother Malcolm tell you that slipping isn't falling? It's not the same. Just as those words they're rapping isn't who they are. But you have the right words. They've been given to you by everyone from Harriet Tubman to Maya Angelou. While you're at it, share some of this with the other young men around you."

"How do I know they'll listen to me?"

"You don't. But what else do you have to do? We're leaders, Terrell.

Leaders influence others. I'm not saying you'll change the world just like that. When I wrote Brenda Has A Baby, do you think I expected to change the whole world? Na, bruh. All we can do as individuals is sprinkle our little seasoning when and where we can."

"Man, it'll take all the seasoning in Food Lion to change the taste of Bad News, VA."

"You got something better to do? Can you think of something better to do? Ok then. You should get to work. Later."

"That's it? I mean, that's all?"

"What else is there? You expecting me to say 'Thug life' or something? Hug life. Do that instead."

Just like that, Tupac was gone. But the following day, a familiar face showed up in class. She was there before Mr. Hail gave us the Penned Influences project, before I even started writing Voices for Choices.

"People will forget what you did, but people will never forget how you made them feel."—Maya Angelou

I still remember how this day made me feel. History class was quieter than usual. It was as if no one was there. Even some of us that were there seemed to be somewhere else. But some of us were there for the first time. Like Shauna. Especially Shauna. She hadn't been to school since getting caught up with Raheem. All those years made her the oldest in class but at least she was in class. When I saw her, I thought it was to speak with her about Raheem and the drugs, a way of redeeming myself for not stepping up for Tawanna. But she was about to receive better help than I could've given her.

"Save the daydreaming for ISS, Shauna. We pursue actual dreams here." said Mr. Wilks.

But Shauna didn't respond. She just sat there. Before I knew it, everyone in class began watching her. That's when I heard the old lady's voice again, but for the very first time, I wasn't alone. Shauna was either just as special or just as crazy as I was.

145

"I know why the caged bird sings," the woman said to her.

Shauna's lips didn't budge in class, but I heard her response clear as day.

"I have no songs to sing."

"There is no greater agony than bearing an untold story inside you. We may encounter many defeats but we must not be defeated. You may not control all the events that happen to you, but you can decide not to be reduced by them. Though you've gone through a horrible storm, you can still become a rainbow in someone's cloud."

"In whose cloud? By now they all know about me."

"People will forget what you did, Shauna. But people will never forget how you made them feel." Make'em feel something, girl."

It definitely made me feel something. I was beginning to understand it. I was beginning to understand all of it. However, Mr. Wilks, who couldn't hear the voices, definitely did not . . .

"Shauna!" he yelled.

"I'm here, Mr. Wilks. I'm sorry, but I'm here."

"Good! Now that we're all in attendance, mentally and physically, it's time we talk about what's coming. With the success of the Hold On program, Mr. Hail is introducing a new idea. The Invisible BFF."

Hearing mummers throughout class wasn't anything new but this was another level.

"The Invisible BFF . . . was is that?"

"Something else to get Brian beat up."

"What do you think, Reverend Brian?"

"This was probably Brian's idea. Pretty soon we'll all be wearing sweater vests and bowties."

They always came for Brian. Being bigger than everyone usually didn't make you the biggest target but being the nicest sometimes did. And that was Brian.

"It doesn't matter what anybody's wearing. This is about being clothed in kindness," Brian said. This boy is never gonna learn to keep his mouth shut, I said to myself. But Brian didn't want to learn our ways. Keeping quiet when it was time to speak up. Standing by when it was time to step in. He didn't want to learn any of our survival skills, the one's I was unlearning.

"So what is the Invisible BFF, Mr. Wilks?"

"It's concept of looking out for each other without each other evening knowing it. Being aware of others. Having each other back."

I hear that, I silently said. Then I heard something that wasn't so silent.

"Our lives begin to end the day we become silent about things that matter."

Then I heard another voice.

"There are two ways of exerting one's strength: one is pushing down, the other is pulling up."

I knew I was meant to repeat them, so finally I did. It had the effect I expected.

"This boy's reciting Shakespeare." said one of my classmates after I was finished.

"Na, that's probably Barack Obama. Y'all don't know? Terrell is running for school president next year."

"Y'all funny, but it's not about that. It's about those who came before us. Those were quotes from Martin Luther King Jr and Booker T. Washington. They were in different times, but time doesn't change some things. Like helping each other. That time is always now."

While I was talking, I saw Mr. Hail and some other teachers walking in. Surprisingly, I was still able concentrate.

"Malcolm X told me, I mean he wrote, "In all our deeds, the proper value and respect for time determines success or failure." This means it has to be now, right now. If you two (Kim and Ayana) don't wanna help pull anyone up, that's on you. But don't put Brian down because he's willing to. Booker T Washington also said, "You can't hold a man down without staying down with him." And I'm not saying we have to get along or agree all the time. No one ever did. A man named W.E.B Du Bois disagreed a lot with Booker T. Washington. He challenged him. But they really wanted the same thing for black people. W.E.B Du Bois said, "There is in this world no such force as the force of a person determined to rise," I believe that now. He also said, "The Talented Tenth of our race must be made leaders of thought and missionaries of culture among their people." Now I don't know exactly what that means, but I know what it doesn't mean. It doesn't mean we get to use each other. It doesn't mean we get to stand by and watch while it happens. And it doesn't mean we get to stay silent when it's time to speak up. . . ."

Before I was finished, I felt a heavy hand on my shoulder. Then the hand spoke, I mean the man spoke—Mr. Hail.

"It means those of us who are gifted must utilize those gifts for the betterment of the recipients—each other. If your talent lies in words or art then pioneer for your generation in a way that requires no apologies. Set standards that aren't substandard. Because as missionaries of our culture, the world will believe you . . . whatever you decide to show them."

Everyone listened when Mr. Hail talked, but everyone still didn't get it.

"Pioneer?" Ayana asked.

"He means doing something first. Doing it right. And taking back our art and turning it into positive culture, music, all of it."

"People can't take back what's already out there. Just look at social media. . . ."

I never thought I would agree with anything Ayana said, but she made sense. How could we undo the negative parts of our culture? That's when Tawanna said something that made a deeper sense.

"People will forget what you did, but people will never forget how you made them feel. When you make a person feel good, they won't research your history or look you up online; they'll just be grateful. If you make positive change, nobody will think about who you used to be. Everybody goes through storms, everyone needs a little sunshine. If this can be that sunshine, I'll do it."

Tawanna was talking to the class but I think she was really talking to Shauna. They didn't know each other but shared experiences has a way connecting people I think.

"Mr. Hail. I want to do it." Tawanna said.

"Me too," I said.

When she looked over at me, it was like my junior high Tawanna was looking at me. And then she smiled.

CHAPTER NINETEEN

Solomon's Song

AS SENIORS WHEN Tawanna, Demetruis, and even Brian got on board with Penned Influences, we started making a real difference. I came up with a 30 day Voices for Choices devotional that used the quotes and ideals of past African American leaders to influence the choices of me and my peers. Mr. Hail was all over it. He loved it. The other teachers loved it too. Hearing the teachers that used to yell at me in frustration now yelling in celebration was crazy. But it was a good crazy, the kind I wanted to get use to. And so did Mr. Hail.

A few days later he called me to his office. When I walked in, there were two other people; one had a camera.

"They are from channel 5 news," he said. "I gave a friend at the city council your book. Now, he wants to give you something.

"A camera . . . ?" I responded. The three of them laughed so I tried to sneak in a chuckle, too.

"A platform, Terrell. That's what I'm talking about. That's what these folks are here for. To record the Penned Influences team interact through the school. See, Terrell, I'm convinced in the power of words; now I'm convinced about you. We're going to convince all of Hampton Roads."

After they left, Mr. Hail grabbed my shoulders and squeezed them as if he was fertilizing them with power. I left there feeling powerful, powerful and anxious. I couldn't wait to tell Mr. Solomon. Being on the news during the daytime was a big deal because we all knew what it meant to be on at night. And my mom, I'd already imagined her fainting at least two times. That was by far the best bus ride home I had that year. The first time my imagination ran wild with optimism until it stopped in the face of reality.

Reality was angry. He looked at me like he'd been waiting for me all day. Reality was Raheem, Phillip's cousin—the drug dealer.

Back when I ran off from his drug spot, somehow he began thinking I ran off some of his drugs also. I didn't. But that didn't matter, not to reality it didn't. Reality already had its mind made up. And no one could reason with it. Not even Mr. Solomon. He knew I didn't steal any drugs, but he also knew it wouldn't matter. I think Solomon knew the whole time. I could tell by the way he rushed me into the house. He didn't follow me in.

"Yo, you need to send him out here. He walked off with something that don't belong to him."

I heard Raheem from inside the house. I tried to listen to everything but she didn't let me.

"The need for change has bulldozed a road down the center of my mind."

Mirrors

I turned around and it was her again, Maya Angelou. She was right. Change was bulldozing a road down the center of my mind, but Mr. Solomon fueled that bulldozer. And at that moment he was outside standing in front of a man holding a gun.

"I can't just be in here," I said.

"You're not just being anything. You're being obedient. Perhaps for the first time. And his last time."

"What? What, who's last time."

As much as I tried, I couldn't hear what was going on outside. I couldn't move either. I was stuck in that awful place of obedience that I both hated and needed.

"Freedom, like all things, is purchased at a cost, Terrell," Sister Angela once said.

"We know the road to freedom has always been stalked by death."

"I don't know what that means," I said while still looking out the window.

"Your bible says;"

"...unless a kernel of wheat falls to the ground and dies, it remains only a single seed. But if it dies, it produces many seeds."

I knew what that meant. As I turned around towards her, I knew it was happening at that moment. Her eyes prepared me for the gun shot before I heard it. But nothing could prepare me to see him lying there. And later seeing him lying in his casket was harder. The more people showed up, the more I realized who Solomon Adi was. Who I was.

"The whole point of being alive is to evolve into the complete person you were intended to be."—Oprah Winfrey

My next day at school was on a Tuesday. No one knew why I was out of school that Monday. No one knew about Mr. Solomon. That was the saddest part. People kept commenting on my improved behavior, but no one knew who to thank for it. Walking in the hallway was the same as always, except Brian was standing by our Penned Influences Board with a big smile on his face.

"What it is?"

"This is change," Brian responded

"We're calling it Mirrors," Tawanna said. "Our way of reading and writing about ourselves until our reflection becomes who we are meant to be."

After they described how they wanted to add their Mirrors concept to my Voices for Choices devotional, I only wished Mr. Solomon could've read it.

"This one came from Oprah." Brian said.

"The whole point of being alive is to evolve into the complete person you were intended to be."

Ms. Winfrey was right. I couldn't see any other reason for Mr. Solomon saving me. So that's what I'm doing now, moving forward into the person I'm intended to be. I'm taking Mr. Solomon with me—the voices, too. And I'm not leaving room for anything else.

The End.

SPECIAL THANKS AND ACKNOWLEDGEMENTS

Woodside High School, Newport News, Virginia
(L.E.P Students and Faculty)

Hoke County Middle School
(Principal McLeod and Faculty)

Yorktown Virginia, Police Department

Yorktown General District Court

Jamison Media LLC

Heather Brower
(Editing)

Vivian Shepherd

Brothers on the Block INC

Restoration Christian Church, Newport News

Tamika Mims

Laquita Lewis

EXET LLC, Newport News

Contributing Images:
Shaun Parker
Tra'Waan Coles
Ashanti Branch
Destiny Burns
Christina "Silky" Burns
Christina W
Armonie Gill
Micah Wormley

155

WORDS FROM THE AUTHOR

FOR MY SON, Andrew Michael Shepherd, and all of tomorrow's leaders who are subjected to the cultural and environmental influences of today.

Become the moral leaders of your own environment. Resist those satisfactions today that may become distasteful tomorrow. Courageously take steps towards integrity and decency, to become pioneers of a new culture. Usher in an uncompromised version of your excellence. Obtain tunnel vision towards all honorable goals. Acquire blinders towards all that would beset you; that you may apply yourself to the fullness of your future self. Compete academically as though you are competing athletically. Then, compete some more.

Compete as though your future depend upon—not winning— but the effort exerted from your willingness to compete. Strive for excellence. Become familiar with it. Become unfamiliar with excuses. Become estranged from anyone with a habit of making them; for such is contagious.

Lastly brothers and sisters, sons and daughters; freedom is the first key to unlocking the doors of opportunity. Turn from any path that lead to potential incarceration. Prison yards remain littered with the fallen branches of our family trees. No more. Know that you are more. Know what you're up against. Now know that even a rigged system isn't an excuse to fail—no more jail.

PENNED INFLUENCES
45 DAYS OF
ENCOURAGEMENT
AND INFLUENCES

Enjoy insight into the ideals that made the voices of
Mirrors legendary.

DAY 1

"I have always tried to be true to myself, to pick those battles I felt were important. My ultimate responsibility is to myself. I could never be anything else."
—*Arthur Ashe.*

"Being true to yourself may not mean being true to the person you are now, but to the person you are meant to be, the person you are designed to be."

"The perception you've created doesn't always reflect the potential behind that creation."

"Many battles we fight seem important to us, but some are only important to who we are now. Who knows who we could become tomorrow?"

#responsibility #future

Little known facts about the author:
Became the first African-American selected to the United States Davis Cup team, won a NCAA singles title and helped UCLA win the NCAA team title.

DAY 2

"Education is the passport to the future,
for tomorrow belongs to those who prepare for it today."
—Malcolm X.

"One must never stop learning. Our current knowledge is only suitable for our current condition."

"A new condition, a new situation, a better future will require newer knowledge."

"There remains a wide door opening towards tomorrow. Many will physically walk through its doorway. But those who've made the mental voyage many times over have already laid their claim."

#learn ahead #stay ahead

Little known facts about the author:
This articulate, passionate, and, naturally gifted leader begun his adulthood in a life of crime.

DAY 3

"*There is in this world no such force as the force of a person determined to rise. The human soul cannot be permanently chained.*"
—*W.E.B. Du Bois*

"If your determination outweighs your fears, if your resolve
can resist the resources of excuses, then your problems
cannot stop your progress."

"A person held down, defeated, or conquered is a person able
to be held down, defeated, and conquered."

#unstoppable #unconquerable

Little known facts about the author:
Considered by many as the most important black protest
leader in the United States during the first half of the
20th century.

DAY 4

"
If you don't like something, change it. If you can't change it,
change your attitude. Don't complain."
—Maya Angelou

"If you dislike something, how long are you willing to dislike it? What have you done to change it?"

"What have you've done to put yourself into position to change it?"

"Turning frustration into positive action is fire worth burning. Without action, it only burns you."

#motivation #passion #action

Little known facts about the author:
Acclaimed Poet and Civil Rights activist chosen to recite poem at President Bill Clinton's inauguration in 1993.

DAY 5

"The freedom to do your best means nothing unless you are willing to do your best."
—Colin Powell

"Don't ask anyone to open a door if you're unready
to walk through it."

"Imagine you only have one shot to reach your goal.
After you reach that goal, imagine you have one shot to
reach the next one."

"Saying 'I'll try harder next time' is believing this is only
practice. This is game time."

#make it count #make every time count

Little known facts about the author:
Colin Powell became the first African American Chairman
of the Joint Chiefs of Staff.

DAY 6

"I prayed for twenty years but received no answer
until I prayed with my legs."
—*Frederick Douglass*

"Hoping and wishing for a situation to change is nothing more than depending on something or someone to change the situation for you."

"You have two legs, two arms, and you have a mind. You have everything you need to change your situation."

#fully equipped #fully empowered

Little known facts about the author:
Though reading was forbidden for slaves, his willingness to risk all for an education made him one of the most famous intellectuals of his time.

DAY 7

"There is no obstacle in the path of young people who are poor or members of minority groups that hard work and preparation cannot cure."
—Barbara Jordan

"If poverty and crime is a disease within your environment, determination and hard work is the cure. A contagious cure."

"This cure lies in the sweat glands of those willing to work their way out of their situations."

#work for it #sweat for it #rise above it all #press toward the mark

Little known facts about the author:
Jordan made history becoming the first African American woman to win a seat in the Texas legislature.

DAY 8

"It is better to be prepared for an opportunity and not have one than to have an opportunity and not be prepared."
—*Whitney Young, Jr.*

"Being ready is being successful.
And time will always prove it."

"Waiting for an opportunity before preparing is waiting to
win the lottery without buying a ticket."

"Successful people aren't chosen by their bosses, coaches, or
teachers. They choose themselves in the off-season when no
one is watching."

#prepare #always prepare #be proactive #be productive
#always abounding

Little known facts about the author:
Appointed executive director of the National Urban League
in 1961 and is credited for opening the eyes of corporate
America towards aid in Civil Rights.

DAY 9

You can't hold a man down without staying down with him.
—Booker T. Washington.

"Your biggest competition is within. Competing against others can take your eyes off your biggest opponent— yourself."

"Never work against anyone. Sabotaging is a method for those lacking optimism in their own trajectory.

Believe in yourself."

"Success isn't a podium, it's a stage. A stage with room for many winners."

#focus on yourself #compete within yourself

Little known facts about the author:
After being chosen as guest speaker to Hampton University graduating classes, Booker T. Washington was chosen to run newly starting Tuskegee University.

DAY 10

"I am what time, circumstance, history, have made of me, certainly, but I am also, much more than that. So are we all."
—*James A. Baldwin*

"You may come from a broken home
but you're much more than that."

"Some may say you're from an inferior race
but you're much more than that."

"Some have preconceived thoughts about you as soon as
you walk into a room, but you're much more than they can
imagine, even more than you can imagine."

"When people fail to see your greatness, pity their vision,
never your reflection."

#divinely designed #destined for greatness

Little known facts about the author:
After moving to Paris in 1948, James Baldwin returned to
the United States in 1957 to become an active voice in the
fight for civil rights.

DAY 11

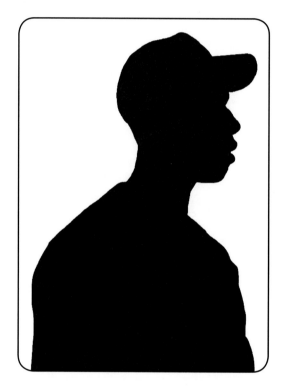

"My motto was always to keep swinging. Whether I was in a slump or feeling badly or having trouble off the field, the only thing to do was keep swinging."
—Hank Aaron

"Keep trying, always keep trying."
"If math is your bat, keep swinging it."

"If science is your bat, keep swinging it."
"You've hit home runs before. You will hit them again."

"Your talent may have seemed to disappear; it hasn't.
It only needs your commitment."

#persistence #dedication #resolute

Little known facts about the author:
Baseball legend who underwent hate and even death threats
on the road to breaking Babe Ruth's homerun record.

DAY 12

"Stumbling is not falling."
—Malcolm X.

"Mistakes can make future winners feel like current failures, but you're still standing."

"You haven't failed. You're not a failure.

You've only taken your eyes off the ball and stumbled, but you're still on your feet."

"Choose to bite down, focus, and regain your balance."

"After you have regained your balanced, look at the things that are making you stumble. Then ask yourself, 'Is this,

is he, is she, are they, worth falling down for?'"

#get up #stand up #stay up

Little known facts about the author:
Though many called Malcolm X radical or violent, he only advocated for justice.

DAY 13

"Ninety-nine percent of the failures come from people who have the habit of making excuses."
—George Washington Carver

"Those who fail are usually weighed down by
pockets full of excuses."

"It is extremely difficult to fail without being ready
to offer a reason why."

"Excuses are escape plans for anyone expecting an easy win."

#no excuses

Little known facts about the author:
Slavery didn't allow George Washington Carver to enter
many school so he used the time in the fields to gain a
fascination for plant life that made him one of the most
famous botanist and inventors of his time.

DAY 14

"There's no free lunch. Don't feel entitled to anything you didn't sweat and struggle for."
—*Marian Wright Edelman*

"If it is given to you, it can be taken from you.

Purchase it with perspiration."

"Unnecessary charity is a wheelchair offered to
a standing man. Accepting it can cause you to sit
and never stand again."

#earn it

Little known facts about the author:
Graduating from Spelman College and Yale Law School in
the mid-60s, Marian Wright Edelman became the first black
woman admitted to the Mississippi Bar.

DAY 15

"In all our deeds, the proper value and respect for time determines success or failure."
—Malcolm X

"The time is now. The time is always now."

"If we need a moment of opportunity, we must be able to act in the very moment of that opportunity or the moment will fade and opportunity will follow."

"Prepare yourself now to walk through the doors that are not yet open."

#no procrastination #lean forward

Little known facts about the author:
The Autobiography of Malcolm X is named by *TIME* magazine one of 10 "required reading" non-fiction books of all-time.

DAY 16

"We should not permit our grievances to overshadow
our opportunity.
—Booker T. Washington

"Teary eyes can produce unclear vision."
"Unclear vision leads to missed opportunities."

"You cannot afford missed opportunities,
as there are no guarantees of second chances."

Little known facts about the author:
In 1872, Booker T. Washington left home and walked 500
miles to Hampton Normal Agricultural Institute in Virginia.

DAY 17

"Everybody wants to do something to help,
but nobody wants to be the first."
—*Pearl Bailey*

"A hero doesn't choose the situation,
the situation chooses the hero."

"Never become more obedient to your fear than you are
to your conscience."

"Leaders step up, sidekicks wait to see if it's safe
to become a hero."

#step up #rise to it

Little known facts about the author:
The Tony and Emmy Award actress and singer was born in
Newport News, Virginia.

DAY 18

*"I had crossed the line. I was free; but there was no one
to welcome me to the land of freedom.
I was a stranger in a strange land."*
—Harriet Tubman

"After achieving your goal there may not be a ceremony or celebration awaiting you, because you've walked the difficult path alone."

"You may realize that after crossing the finish line, you may not recognize any of the other winners. And that is ok."

"Winners will soon recognize each other. Your time as a winner will be much longer than your time as a stranger."

#humility

Little known facts about the author:
The first woman to lead an armed expedition in the war, Harriet Tubman guided the Combahee River Raid, which liberated more than 700 slaves in South Carolina.

DAY 19

"Start where you are. Use what you have. Do what you can."
—*Arthur Ashe*

"If inferior tools and resources are at your disposal right now, use them to show your superior willingness to excel."

"Do everything in your power until your power increases."

#victor #conqueror

Little known facts about the author:
Was a World No. 1 ranked professional tennis player.
He won three Grand Slam titles.

DAY 20

"Jails and prisons are designed to break human beings, to convert the population into specimens in a zoo—obedient to our keepers, but dangerous to each other."
—Angela Davis

"Understand what you're up against."
"Understand the consequences."

"Cages were designed for animals.
You were designed for greatness."

#uncaged #unchained #unstoppable

Little known facts about the author:
After rumored association with the Blank Panther party,
Angela Davis still became a college professor at the
University of California, Santa Cruz

DAY 21

"The world cares very little about what a man or woman knows; it is what a man or woman is able to do that counts."
—*Booker T. Washington*

"The story you tell with your hands is easier to believe than the story you tell with your lips."

"Never sit on knowledge as if having it is enough.

An unplanted harvest will never produce."

#action #results

Little known facts about the author:
Became a Presidential advisor although being born into slavery in Virginia

DAY 22

"It's not the load that breaks you down,
it's the way you carry it."
—Lena Horne

"Your responsibilities are heavy, and they may seem unfair.
But you stand tall and use the strength you were given."

"Your strength of character will support this load."
"And the next load."

#stand tall #stand strong #endure

Little known facts about the author:
Lena Horne carried the load of racism and biases as the only
black performer in her earlier performance groups.

DAY 23

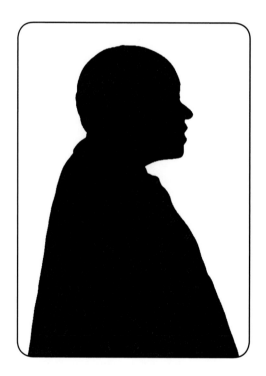

*"My whole life, my whole soul,
my whole spirit is to blow that horn."*
—*Music Legend, Louis Armstrong*

"Dedicate yourself to your craft until your craft becomes
a reflection of you."

"Whatever you choose to do, make it more than just
something you do—make it who you are."

"Submerge yourself into your talents until you arise a perfect
representation of those talents."

#passion #focus #expression

Little known facts about the author:
This music legend overcame a fatherless home and a mother
given to prostitution to become a renowned iconic musician.

DAY 24

"Never underestimate the power of dreams and the influence of the human spirit. We are all the same in this notion: The potential for greatness lives within each of us."
—Wilma Rudolph

"There's a seed of greatness in all of us."
"Encourage it to grow in yourself."

"Then encourage the person next to you."

#Strength #courage #fortitude

Little known facts about the author:
This Olympic legend wasn't able to walk on her own until
the age of twelve, due to premature birth.

DAY 25

"*The need for change bulldozed road down the center of my mind.*"
—*Maya Angelou*

"Changing isn't quitting on the person you are today;
it is committing to the person you will be tomorrow."

"It takes courage to choose your own path but it takes genius
to accept that a different path is needed."

Little known facts about the author:
Before becoming the poetic voice of civil justice and equality,
Maya Angelou refused to speak for a number of years after
being sexually assaulted as a child.

DAY 26

*"Our lives begin to end the day we become silent
about things that matter."*
—Martin Luther King, Jr.

"If your 'eyes are windows into your soul,' how can you
ignore what comes past your window? How can you ignore
what you see? Or what you hear? Or what you learn."

"Your soul thrives by the crosses you chose to pick up."
"It dies by the ones you chose to leave on the ground"

#courageous #humanity

Little known facts about the author:
This civil rights leader received his Doctorate degree from
Boston University at 25 years of age.

DAY 27

"Believe me, the reward is not so great without the struggle."
—Wilma Rudolph

"What makes something worth having is the effort it takes to have it."

"Some rewards you receive for being there; other rewards you receive for being the best one there. Sweat and sacrifice separate the two prizes."

Little known facts about the author:
Wilma Rudolph became the first American woman to win three gold medals in track and field at a single Olympics in 1960.

DAY 28

"Whoever said anybody has a right to give up?"
—Marian Wright Edelman

"Quitting is a permission we THINK we have, but we don't."

"Your talent and abilities were purchased with an unwritten
obligation to never stop trying—an obligation
to your creator."

"Don't stop; beginning is the hardest part. The rest is only
moving one foot forward after the other."

#perseverance

Little known facts about the author:
In 1973, to defend poor, minority and handicapped children,
Marian Wright Edelman established the Children's Defense
Fund (CDF).

DAY 29

"I tire so of hearing people say, let things take their course.
Tomorrow is another day. I do not need my freedom when I'm
dead. I cannot live on tomorrow's bread."
—*Langston Hughes*

"If you're prepared now, and the opportunity is now, then the time is now."

"Waiting for another opportunity tomorrow is believing today is only a rehearsal. Today counts, today always counts."

"The opportunity of a lifetime depends solely on the lifetime of that specific opportunity."

#inquire #ask #act

Little known facts about the author:
When African American communities were often seen as criminal and inferior, Langston Hughes became the leading voice of the Harlem Renaissance, whose poetry depicted the dignity and beauty of ordinary black life.

DAY 30

"Why is it that, as a culture, we are more comfortable seeing two men holding guns than holding hands?"
—*Ernest Gaines*

"The bond of brotherhood is only severed when we let go of each other."

"Do you not consider it strange to need your brother; consider it a gain to have one."

"Consider it a loss to lose one."

#brotherhood

Little known facts about author:
Ernest Gaines was interested in literature from an early age but unable to find any African American literature to learn from, so he began creating his own.

DAY 31

"People come out to see you perform and you've got to give them the best you have within you."
—*Jesse Owens*

"No one owes you their support, but you owe your supporters the best you have to give."

"Repay their time and attendance with effort and more effort."

"Cheating those who support you cuts deep; cheating yourself cuts deeper. Find the winner within."

#appreciation #reciprocation

Little known facts about the author:
Born the grandson of slaves, young Jesse Owens was picking up to 100 pounds of cotton a day to help his family put food on the table.

DAY 32

*"The whole point of being alive is to evolve into the complete
person you were intended to be."*
—Oprah Winfrey

"Who is here just to be here? Who is here because it's their turn? Who's here by mistake?

"You're here for a reason. You may not know the reason, but if you fail to give each day your very best, you may never know the reason."

"Become who you were created to become. You were placed in these circumstances and situations for that reason."

#purpose

Little known facts about the author:
Before championing education for young girls in South Africa, Oprah Winfrey overcame sexual abuse as a child.

DAY 33

"I tire so of hearing people say, let things take their course.
Tomorrow is another day. I do not need my freedom when I'm
dead. I cannot live on tomorrow's bread."
—*Langston Hughes*

"The time is now, the time is always now."

"If you're prepared and the opportunity is there, take it."

"Waiting for another opportunity tomorrow is believing today is only a rehearsal. Today counts, today always counts."

#inquire #ask #act

Little known facts about the author:
When African American communities were often seen as criminal and inferior, Langston Hughes became the leading voice of the Harlem Renaissance, whose poetry depicted the dignity and beauty of ordinary black life.

DAY 34

"The worker must work for the glory of his handiwork, not simply for pay; the thinker must think for truth, not for fame."
—*W.E.B. Du Bois*

"If applause is your motivation, the audience owns you."
"If money is your motivation, your company owns you."

"When doing a great job motivates you, your talent owns
you. And you will own your talent."

#pride

Little known facts about the author:
Though hindered by Jim Crow laws, W.E.B. Du Bois became
the first African American to earn a Ph.D. from Harvard
University in 1895.

DAY 35

"I always wanted to be somebody. If I made it, it's half because I was game enough to take a lot of punishment along the way and half because there were a lot of people who cared enough to help me."
—Althea Gibson

"Knowing what you want is one thing, learning how much you really want is another."

"No one can want it (success) for you, you must want it for yourself."

"The help you receive from loved ones is only to balance out the hardships that you will encounter; but the wanting and doing will always be up to you."

#destiny #desire

Little known facts about the author:
In a time of intense of prejudices, Althea Gibson's talents made her the first African American athlete (man or woman) invited to Wimbledon.

DAY 36

"A little less complaint and whining, and a little more dogged work and manly striving, would do us more credit than a thousand civil rights bills."
—*W.E.B. Du Bois*

"When the odds are against you, remember what it takes to even them . . . hard work, dedication, and no excuses."

"You want things to be fair and they should be, but you don't need them to be. You can overcome it."

"Uphill battles are difficult, but they strengthen your legs for challenges to come. Everything is preparing you for something else."

#overcome #overachieve

Little known facts about the author:
W.E.B. Du Bois was one of the creators of the National Association for the Advancement of Colored People (NAACP).

DAY 37

"Truth burns up error."
—Sojourner Truth

"When one's offense may seem unforgivable; the warmth of honesty may melt away the icy repercussions.

"Turning from your mistaken behavior can set fire to the past you wish to forget. And no one can identify the ashes."

#humility

Little known facts about the author:
When her child was illegally sold by slave owners, Sojourner Truth became one of the first African Americans to win a slave case in an American court.

DAY 38

*"You should always know when you're shifting gears in life.
You should leave your era; it should never leave you."*
—*Leontyne Price*

"Lead your generation into the future, but be prepared to leave some of your generation in the past."

"If Monday is around the corner,
begin preparing for Tuesday."

#lead #pioneer

Little known facts about the author:
This famous opera singer began by studying to be a music teacher but believing in her talent, she changed her focus to singing. The rest was history.

DAY 39

"We know the road to freedom has always been stalked by death."
—*Angela Davis*

"Choosing the harsh path that others are unprepared for will cause others to speak harsh of you. Ignore them."

"Those without vision will always seek comfort in the destruction of your dreams."

Little known facts about the author:
Angela Davis ran for U.S. Vice President on the Communist Party ticket in 1980.

DAY 40

"Those that don't got it, can't show it.
Those that got it, can't hide it."
—Zora Neale Hurston

"Confidence is a candle that doesn't need
to be continuously lit."

"It is a muscle that doesn't need to be flexed."
"It is a lion that doesn't need to roar"

"Once forged by preparation, confidence just needs
to be confident."

Little known facts about the author:
Zora Neale Hurston's famed novel, *Their Eyes Were Watching
God*, was made into a movie starring Halle Berry in 2005.

DAY 41

"I have never had much patience with the multitudes of people
who are always ready to explain why one cannot succeed.
I have always had high regard for the man who could tell me
how to succeed.
—Booker T. Washington

"The world is one of various waters. Some still oceans, others roaring rivers. The oceans cry loud throughout the night but remain still in the daylight. But rivers run and rivers roar both day and night. Likewise, large bodies of people cry out at night but remain still in the opportunity of daylight. But the smaller rivers, like you, are just as active as they are loud.

Be a river. Run as often as you roar. Never sit still in the opportunity of daylight."

Little known facts about the author:
This social and educational leader was often and heavily critics by African Americans for his, "earn respect instead of demanding respect" approach to equality.

DAY 42

"Success is a journey not a destination.
The doing is usually more important than the outcome."
—Arthur Ashe

"Winning is beginning."

"The most important experiences are gained during the journey, not after."

"If you focus on going places in life, you'll never regret where you end up."

#win #begin

Little known facts about the author:
To better prepare minorities for life after sports, Arthur Ashe advocated for higher academic standards for athletes.

DAY 43

"You've got to get to the stage in life where going for it is more important than winning or losing."
—Arthur Ashe.

"Success doesn't come when your feet cross the finish line.
It comes when they leave the starting line."

""Never allow doubt or uncertainty to stop you from taking
a leap of faith—believe in yourself and go for it."

"Don't worry about how you finish the race;
starting is the key."

#take a chance #then take another chance

Little known facts about the author:
Arthur Ashe was the first and only African American
to win Wimbledon.

DAY 44

"We must reinforce argument with results."
—*Booker T. Washington*

"Anyone can point out a problem, but replacing blame with solutions are what leaders are made of."

"The world is filled with debaters. Classrooms, school buses, and locker rooms are all filled with the opinions of spectators. But the world isn't in need of more spectators, but more operators, creators, and innovators. Chose the latter and you will climb many ladders."

#less talking #more walking

Little known facts about the author:
Though born into slavery in Virginia, he became the chief African American advisor to both President Roosevelt and his successor, President William Howard Taft.

DAY 45

"Believe me, the reward is not so great without the struggle."
—*Wilma Rudolph*

"What makes something worth having is the effort it takes to have it."

"Some rewards you receive for being there; other rewards you receive for being the best one there. Sweat and sacrifice separate the two prizes."

#pursue #persevere

Little known facts about the author:
Wilma Rudolph became the first American woman to win three gold medals in track and field at a single Olympics in 1960.

CITATIONS

1. Arthur Ashe (July 10, 1943 – Feb 06, 1993) "I have always tried to be true to myself, to pick those battles I felt were important. My ultimate responsibility is to myself. I could never be anything else." (http://www.quotesigma.com/57-motivating-quotes-by-arthur- ashe/) March 12, 2015

   "Start where you are. Use what you have. Do what you can." (http://www.great-quotes.com/quotes/author/Arthur/Ashe) Copyright

   © 2002-2013 Great Quotes.com

   "Success is a journey not a destination. The doing is usually more important than the outcome." (http://quotationsbook.com/quote/37558/)

   "You've got to get to the stage in life where going for it is more important than winning or losing." (https://www.brainyquote.com/quotes/arthur_ashe_154562)

   "From what we get, we can make a living; what we give, however, makes a life." (https://www.passiton.com/inspirational-quotes/3059-from-what-we-get-we-can-make-a-living-what-we)

   "Clothes and manners do not make the man; but when he is made, they greatly improve his appearance." (https://www.brainyquote.com/quotes/arthur_ashe_119072)

"If you're paid before you walk on the court, what's the point in playing as if your life depended on it?" (https://www.brainyquote.com/quotes/arthur_ashe_387032)

2. Malcolm X (May 19, 1925 – Feb 21, 1965) "Education is the passport to the future, for tomorrow belongs to those who prepare for it today." (https://www.goodreads.com/quotes/788-education-is-our-passport-to-the-future-for-tomorrow-belongs)

"Stumbling is not falling." (http://malcolmx.com/quotes/) © 2015. The Estate of Malcolm X

"In all our deeds, the proper value and respect for time determines success or failure." (http://www.quotes-inspirational.com/quote/our-deeds-proper-value-respect-98/)

3. W.E.B. Du Bois (February 23, 1868 – 1763) "There is in this world no such force as the force of a person determined to rise. The human soul cannot be permanently chained." (http://www.doonething.org/heroes/pages-d/dubois-quotes.htm)

"The worker must work for the glory of his handiwork, not simply for pay; the thinker must think for truth, not for fame." (http://izquotes.com/quote/225467)

"A little less complaint and whining, and a little more dogged work and manly striving, would do us more credit than a thousand civil rights bills." (https://quizlet.com/18750380/early-civil-rights-leaders-flash-cards/)

4. Maya Angelou (April 04, 1928 – May 28, 2014) "If you don't like something, change it. If you can't change it, change your attitude. Don't complain." (https://michaelhyatt.com/photos/dont-like-something-change-cant-change-change-attitude-dont-complain-maya-angelou/) 2017

"The need for change bulldozed a road down the center of my mind." (http://quotationsbook.com/quote/5603/) © MMVII Quotations Book

"I know why the caged bird sings," (http://www.sparknotes.com/lit/cagedbird/)

"There is no greater agony than bearing an untold story inside you." (https://www.brainyquote.com/quotes/maya_angelou_133956)

"We may encounter many defeats but we must not be defeated." (https://www.brainyquote.com/quotes/maya_angelou_165173)

"You may not control all the events that happen to you, but you can decide not to be reduced by them." (www.theseeds4life.com › All Seeds)

"...become a rainbow in someone's cloud." (https://www.brainyquote.com/quotes/maya_angelou_578763)

"People will forget what you did, but people will never forget how you made them feel." (https://www.brainyquote.com/quotes/maya_angelou_392897)

5. Colin Powell (April 5, 1937 – Present) "The freedom to do your best means nothing unless you are willing to do your best." (https://www.goodreads.com/quotes/26893-the-freedom-to-do-your-best-means-nothing-unless-you)

"I'm not perfect but I'll be the creator of perfection." (https://www.goodreads.com/author/quotes/138507.colin _powell)

6. Frederick Douglass (February 1818 – February 20, 1895) "I prayed for twenty years but received no answer until I prayed with my legs." (http://thinkexist.com/quotation/i_prayed_for_twenty_years_but_received_no_answer/205929.html)

"It is easier to build strong children than to repair broken men" (https://www.brainyquote.com/quotes/frederick_douglass_201574)

7. Barbara Jordan (Feb 21, 1936 - Jan 17, 1996) "There is no obstacle in the path of young people who are poor or members of minority groups that hard work and preparation cannot cure." (https://www.goodreads.com/author/quotes/385332.Barbara _Jordan)

8. Whitney Young, Jr (Jul 31, 1921 - Mar 11, 1971) "It is better to be prepared for an opportunity and not have one than to have an opportunity and not be prepared." (http://www.searchquotes.com/search/Whitney_Young_Jr/)

9. Booker T. Washington (Apr 05, 1856 - Nov 14, 1915) "You can't hold a man down without staying down with him. (https://www.goodreads.com/author/quotes/84278.Booker_T_Washington)

"We should not permit our grievances to overshadow our opportunity."(http://www.btwsociety.org/library/misc/quotes. php)

"The world cares very little about what a man or woman knows; it is what a man or woman is able to do that counts." (https://www.goodreads.com/author/quotes/84278.Booker_T_Washington) © 2017 Goodreads Inc

"I have never had much patience with the multitudes of people who are always ready to explain why one cannot succeed. I have always had high regard for the man who could tell me how to succeed." (https://www.poetrysoup.com/quotes/multitudes)

"We must reinforce argument with results." (https://www.quotes-inspirational.com/quote/reinforce-argument-results-63/

"There are two ways of exerting one's strength: one is pushing down, the other is pulling up." (https://www.brainyquote.com/quotes/booker_t_washington_133740)

"I have learned that success is to be measured not so much by the position that one has reached in life as by the obstacles which he has had to overcome while trying to succeed" (https://www.brainyquote.com/quotes/booker_t_washington_139251)

"Let us keep before us the fact that, almost without exception, every race or nation that has ever got upon its feet has done so through struggle and trial and persecution; and out of this very resistance to wrong, out of the struggle against odds, they have gained strength, self-confidence, and experience which they could not have gained in any other way." < African American Political Thought, 1890-1930: Washington, Du Bois, Garvey, and Randolph. Edited By Cary D. Wintz>

Associate yourself with people of good quality, for it is better to be alone than in bad company."

"No one can degrade us except ourselves." (https://www.brainy quote.com/quotes/booker_t_washington_130024)

"No one can degrade us except ourselves." (https://quotefancy. com/quote/777367/Booker-T-Washington-No-one-can...)

10. James A. Baldwin (Aug 02, 1924 - Dec 01, 1987) "I am what time, circumstance, history, have made of me, certainly, but I am also, much more than that. So are we all." (http://www.great-quotes. com/quotes/author/james/baldwin) Copyright © 2002-2013 Great Quotes.com

11. Hank Aaron (Feb 05, 1934 – Present) "My motto was always to keep swinging. Whether I was in a slump or feeling badly or having trouble off the field, the only thing to do was keep swinging." (http://www.great-quotes.com/quotes/author/Hank/ Aaron) Copyright © 2002-2013 Great Quotes.com

12. George Washington Carver (1861 - Jan 05, 1943) "Ninety-nine percent of the failures come from people who have the habit of making excuses." (https://www.goodreads.com/author/quotes/1495762.George_Washington_Carver) © 2017 Goodreads Inc

13. Marian Wright Edelman (Jun 06, 1939 – Present) "There's no free lunch. Don't feel entitled to anything you didn't sweat and struggle for." (https://msu.edu/user/stromsco/edelman.html)

    "Whoever said anybody has a right to give up?" (http://www.quotes-inspirational.com/quote/whoever-said-anybody-right-give-68/)

14. Pearl Bailey (Mar 29, 1918 – Aug 17, 1990) "Everybody wants to do something to help, but nobody wants to be the first." (http://www.searchquotes.com/quotes/author/Pearl_Bailey/2/)

15. Harriet Tubman (1822 – Mar 10, 1913) "I had crossed the line. I was free; but there was no one to welcome me to the land of freedom. I was a stranger in a strange land." (http://www.great-quotes.com/quotes/author/Harriet/Tubman)

16. Angela Davis (Jan 26, 1944 – Present) "Jails and prisons are designed to break human beings, to convert the population into specimens in a zoo - obedient to our keepers, but dangerous to each other." (http://www.searchquotes.com/quotes/author/angeladavis)

    "We know the road to freedom has always been stalked by death." (http://www.quotes-inspirational.com/quote/know-road-freedom-been-stalked-76/)

17. Lena Horne (Jun 30, 1917 – May 09, 2010) "It's not the load that breaks you down, it's the way you carry it." (https://www.goodreads.com/author/quotes/158428.Lena_Horne) © 2017 Goodreads Inc

18. Louis Armstrong (Aug 04, 1901 - Jul 06, 1971) "My whole life, my whole soul, my whole spirit is to blow that horn." (http://www.great-quotes.com/quotes/author/louis/armstrong)

19. Wilma Rudolph (Jun 23, 1940 – Nov 12, 1994) "Never underestimate the power of dreams and the influence of the human spirit. We are all the same in this notion: The potential for greatness lives within each of us." (http://www.great-quotes.com/quotes/author/Wilma/Rudolph)

    "Believe me, the reward is not so great without the struggle." (http://www.great-quotes.com/quotes/author/Wilma/Rudolph)

20. Martin Luther King, Jr. (Jan 15, 1929 – Apr 04, 1968) "Our lives begin to end the day we become silent about things that matter." (https://www.goodreads.com/author/quotes/23924.Martin_Luther_King_Jr_)

21. Langston Hughes (Feb 01, 1902 – May 22, 1967) "I tire so of hearing people say, let things take their course. Tomorrow is another day. I do not need my freedom when I'm dead. I cannot live on tomorrow's bread." (http://famouspoetsandpoems.com/poets/langston_hughes/poems/16957)

22. Ernest Gaines (January 15, 1933 – Present) "Why is it that, as a culture, we are more comfortable seeing two men holding guns than holding hands?" (https://www.goodreads.com/quotes/213177-why-is-it-that-as-a-culture-we-are-more)

23. Jesse Owens (Sep 12, 1913 – Mar 31, 1980) "People come out to see you perform and you've got to give them the best you have within you." (http://www.jesseowens.com/quotes/)

24. Oprah Winfrey (Jan 29, 1954 – Present) "The whole point of being alive is to evolve into the complete person you were intended to be." ("The whole point of being alive is to evolve into the complete person you were intended to be.")

25. Althea Gibson (Aug 25, 1927 – Sep 28, 2003) "I always wanted to be somebody. If I made it, it's half because I was game enough to take a lot of punishment along the way and half because there were a lot of people who cared enough to help me." (https://www.thoughtco.com/althea-gibson-3529144)

26. Sojourner Truth (1797 – Nov 26, 1883) "Truth burns up error. "(https://www.thoughtco.com/sojourner-truth-quotes-3530178)

27. Leontyne Price (Feb 10, 1927 – Present) "You should always know when you're shifting gears in life. You should leave your era; it should never leave you." (https://www.lifesayingsquotes.com/quotes/shifting/)

28. Zora Neale Hurston (Jan 07, 1891 – Jan 28, 1960) "Those that don't got it, can't show it. Those that got it, can't hide it. "(https://quoteinvestigator.com/2013/11/06/got-it/)

29. Richard Wright (Sep 04, 1908 - Nov 28, 1960) "The impulse to dream was slowly beaten out of me by experience. Now it surged up again and I hungered for books, new ways of looking and seeing." (https://www.brainyquote.com/quotes/richard_wright_406704)

30. Rae Sremmurd / Nicki Minaj, "The more you spend it, the faster it go Bad bitches, on the floor, its rainin' hunnids Throw some mo', throw some mo'" (https://www.azlyrics.com/lyrics/raesremmurd/throwsummo.html)

31. Tupac Shakur (Jun 16, 1971 – Sep 13, 1996) "Reality is wrong. Dreams are for real." (https://www.brainyquote.com/quotes/tupac_shakur_100941)

""I got love for my brother, but we can never go nowhere unless we share with each other. We gotta start makin' changes. Learn to see me as a brother 'stead of 2 distant strangers. And that's how it's supposed to be. How can the Devil take a brother if he's close to me? I'd love to go back to when we played as kids but things changed, and that's the way it is." . . . I see no changes. All I see is racist faces. Misplaced hate makes disgrace to races, we under, I wonder what it takes to make this one better place . . . let's erase the wasted." (https://www.azlyrics.com/lyrics/2pac/changes.html)

32. Kanye West ". . . you need to crawl before you ball, come and meet me in the bathroom stall, and show me why you deserve to have it all . . ." https://www.azlyrics.com/lyrics/kanyewest/niggasinparis.html

33. Shawn Carter / Jay Z ("I'm not afraid of dying, I'm afraid of not trying, Everyday hit every wave like I'm Hawaiian." (https://www.azlyrics.com/lyrics/jayz/beachchair.html)

34. John 12:24, New International Version (NIV) "unless a kernel of wheat falls to the ground and dies, it remains only a single seed. But if it dies, it produces many seeds."